To Patty

Carolina Comfort II

Karen Dodd

Karen Dodd

Published by:

Karen Dodd
6304 Albatross Drive
New Bern, NC 28560

dkdodd1@ cox.net

ISBN: 0-9707197-2-8

Carolina Comfort II

First Edition

Acknowledgements

A group of writers led by Maxine Harker meets weekly in New Bern, NC. They read, critique, praise, discard, or designate saleable each manuscript. I've enjoyed being a part of the group. Thank you to Shirley Blackwell, Eileen Cella, Nancy Cook, Doris Dyson, Sara Howell, Andy Jones, Ivan Marty, Jerome Norris, Edwina Rooker, Ruth Russell, Betsy Sprague, Glenda Wilkins, and Flora Ann Scearce.

My daughter, Christine Grotheer, husband, Denton Dodd, and Rosalie Wood edited these words. If there are errors or omissions, I take full responsibility.

The memoirs are my recollections. The short stories are fiction, a product of my imagination and not meant to be otherwise.

- The author's photograph for the back cover was taken by Carl Hultman.

TABLE OF CONTETS

MEMOIRS

LITTLE GIRL

The first year, you lived by the ocean in the shade of Hatteras Light, where seagulls soared above your head and wild ponies trotted across your backyard. Daddy shot a deer and hung the hide on the outhouse wall to keep the winter winds from whistling through the cracks. Mama hung clothes on the back yard line and ponies snuffled nearby. Like your Mama, who killed a copperhead on her back steps, you braved challenges without a whimper.

Mostly, you wanted a pony of your own, hung around your big sister, loved candy, and played your favorite records. After a stint on the Outer Banks, Daddy transferred to New London, CT to teach at the CG Telephone School. Your record player played constantly. Singing and dancing to the music, you performed across the stair landing of the two-story duplex.

Your nickname was Kicker. You kicked a lot, whether it was during diaper changes when you were younger or later as you stomped around in your cowboy boots. Back then, you and your big sister were inseparable -- until she found out she didn't have to take you everywhere. Then you pouted. That nickname died the same day as your big sister.

When your parents went away on vacation, the babysitter baked potatoes for supper. That was the first time you ever had one. You mashed butter and green peas into the steaming white center, then gobbled it up. Food was an important part of your life. Food meant family togetherness, celebrations, reward, and comfort.

You wanted to be a cowboy. At the prime age of three, you wrapped your cherished possessions into a bandana sack, tied it to a stick and walked with your sister, whose idea it was in the first place, in below-freezing weather to the turnpike to hitch a ride out west! Unbeknown to you both, Mama followed a block behind in the

Oldsmobile until you were too cold to go any farther. Hot chocolate was your reward for coming home.

Mama read to you, your sister, and now, the brother every night. Uncle Wiggily, Grimm's Fairy Tales, Black Beauty, and Childcraft stories led you to the tales of Nancy Drew, Black Stallion, and Admiral Sperry. Books were your escape.

You loved horses. Daddy knew the real Mr. Beebe and other characters in your favorite book, Misty of Chincoteague. Thirty years later as a young single parent, you bought five acres of land and built a house with the intention of finally getting a horse. The University of Florida accepted your application to the doctorate program. Giving up your horse forever, you went back to college, again.

Except for your clomping, you were a quiet, shy, but happy child. You played by yourself after being deserted by your big sister. It wasn't until you were in high school that you tried to be outgoing. You ran for office, and lost. You tried out for parts, but didn't get them. Disappointment in not living up to your older sister's standard didn't dissolve until you left home.

Your red hair faded into dirty blond then grew into a rich sable brown, identical to both your sisters'. Yep, you got a little sister when you were in high school, but she was too young to play with until she grew up.

Fifty years later your granddaughter's dark red hair surprised everyone. Your grandson's hair glints red in the sun. You never stopped clinging to things like family and friends. A family reunion called you back to visit a cousin recently. Her back yard edges a neighbor's pasture. Reading the morning paper on her back porch -- you rediscovered the pleasure of hearing a horse's snuffle.

IT'S CALLED A STATION WAGON

"It's called a station wagon," he cackled, "and it's our new car!" My father and Uncle Henderson had pulled the green 1954 Chevrolet into Granny's yard and hollered for Mama and all of us to come see. He threw back his head and laughed at Mama's face. She had one of those surprised O-mouthed expressions that caused her eyebrows to climb up into her bangs.

Uncle Henderson had retired after thirty years of driving for Greyhound and was selling cars at LaPoint Chevrolet in Charlotte. I guess he needed another sale for the month and true to Grandfather's horse-trading legacy, talked Daddy into trading our 1949 black two-door Oldsmobile, without any input from Mama.

Back then, as now, Gaston County was a dry county and I'm sure the deal got struck in a little bar just over the Mecklenburg County line, where my Daddy and his brothers met most Saturdays when we visited. Daddy, liquor on his breath, felt mighty good about the swap until he saw

Mama's lips tighten and her fists notch in at her waist.

He beckoned to Mama, my big sister, Junior, Granny, my aunts, cousins and me, "Come see all the features." He folded down the black and white plastic seats and showed how both back seats could lie flat with a little side seat independent of the middle bench. He took Mama around and let her sit on the driver's side and see how easy it was to shift gears on the column. Daddy let us honk the horn, crawl over the rear drop-down door and practice stretching out in back. By this time we kids had inhaled enough new car smell to become addicted to the station wagon and all its features.

Up until that time, my sister and I had to lie head to toe in the back seat sleeping on the long trips between where we lived and Mt. Holly. Mama usually held Junior or wedged him between them both up front. Now we could all three sleep in the back while they drove and we still had room for suitcases at our feet.

An even better argument by Daddy was that we could take vacation trips camping out along the way. Charlie Rich might have had my parents in mind when he wrote the lyrics to "Behind Closed Doors" because by the next morning the station wagon had received approval from the whole family.

Over the next thirty years, we traded into four different station wagons and traveled from Nova Scotia to St. Augustine, from Hatteras to Anaheim, back and forth to five college campuses, helped move four kids into and out of a total of eleven residences and more trips to Granny's house six hours away, than I care to count. We had camped in the Great Smokies, cooked breakfast in New Mexico, boiled lobsters in Massachusetts, pitched a tent on the Outer Banks, and had the mosquito bites to prove it.

We sometimes stayed in motels. Mama attacked those bathrooms with Lysol and Ajax, searched for bugs, pulled down the bedspreads and folded over the sheets before we kids could get out of the car. Because of those station wagons, we could pull over to the side of the road and scramble eggs on a Coleman stove, store sandwich meats and Daddy's beer in an ice chest, nap or play checkers and "auto bingo" in the back. Daddy even figured out how to heat pork'n beans and corned beef under the car hood as we traveled. Of course, one time he didn't make the hole big enough in the can and it blew dinner all over the engine. It smelled pretty good for a while, but you can imagine the look on the service station attendant's face as he checked the oil after filling up our gas tank.

Nothing can accurately describe the good times and terrors we've had traveling in those station wagons. You couldn't tell Daddy not to pick up hitchhikers. He picked up the "boys" because he felt sorry for them not having a car. Mama would squash herself into the center seat, sometimes holding her breath in fear of being killed by thumb-wielding vagabonds or -- so she could avoid his body stench. We kids would drop back on our seat with our hands holding our noses or roll down the window.

After letting someone in the car Daddy'd ask where he was headed. Daddy usually talked. He was a great storyteller. Sometimes it was from Morehead City to Beaufort but I can remember one time we were driving to Charlotte from Groton, Connecticut where we lived at the time. We repeatedly saw a young sailor in pea jacket hefting his duffle bag. We'd pass him and then we'd see him again where some trucker left him. We finally picked him up in snowy Pennsylvania and took him to Charlotte for his Christmas leave! Mama didn't mind that so much.

Daddy was still driving at 78 when he came home late one evening after a haircut. When Mama asked him what kept him, he just scratched his head. A stranger at the Morehead Plaza noticed the retired Coast Guard sticker on our car, said he was a Coastie and asked Daddy for a ride back to Ft. Macon! Daddy took him. People who knew my father knew he'd do anything for them -- all they had to do was ask.

Daddy also had a fascination with snakes. As soon as he'd see one zigzagging across the highway, he'd jump out with a burlap bag and grab that snake's tail then throw the writhing bag in the back of the car. Sometimes he'd take them to show the men at work, give them to the neighborhood "naturalist," Bob Simpson, or let them loose again. I saw them go in the bag but never saw them come out! Daddy liked snakes and wanted to know all about them. To this day

I can't even look at a snake's picture without goose bumps crawling up my neck. I break out in a cold sweat if I see something wriggling in a tow sack.

We've all grown up and got kids of our own and some of us have grandchildren. None of us every owned a station wagon, nor did we take our kids camping as far as I can recall. My older sister built a log cabin and retreated to the North Carolina mountains. My camping days converted to living aboard our boat the past few years. My younger sister raised and trained a plethora of animals from baby ducks to prizewinning dressage horses and Sam Jr. lives in a respectable two-story house near Bogue Sound. I'm afraid none of us got the station wagon fervor.

In later years Mama took over my parent's finances. She called me up one day to go car shopping. Dodge had come out with something that caught her eye and she wanted me to tag along to play Devil's advocate with the car salesman. This new vehicle was roomy, had lots of cubbyholes for storage, could load up a bunch of suitcases and yard sale stuff, carry all the grandkids to the beach, and had a little running board that made it easier for her to climb behind the wheel. After taking it for a test drive, we drove it home. Daddy came in from work, driving his two-tone brown station wagon, in time to find us climbing out of her new vehicle.

She threw back her head and pointed to the sliding side door and said, "It's called a van, Sam. Let me show you the features."

First printed in *The Rambler Magazine*, July-August, 2005.

DON'T ASK ME HOW I KNOW

My grandmother taught us by doing -- not telling. I watched her sweep dried leaves and geranium blossoms off the front porch. She flicked the broom straw, whisking dirt and fallen planticles from corners. Her chubby hands gripped the cow's teat, making a steady ping against the side of the white enamel bucket. Smells of hay and cow tickled my nose as I stood looking over her shoulder. Distracted from her storytelling by the kittens mewing in the corner, I felt a shot of warm milk in my face. She cackled, pointing her short finger at me. After covering the frothing bucket, we'd cross the road back home to divide the milk into dark glazed pitchers. *Grocery stores today offer a wide selection of "milk." You get confused reading the ingredients on the carton.*

"Did you get the eggs in yet?" The tip of her tongue escaped her lips waiting for my answer.

"That ol' red hen pecks at me, Granny. I don't like going in there." I turned up my nose, remembering the ripe odor of soured milk, scraps in the feed pan and chicken house poop. She never bothered arguing but grabbed up the wire basket and motioned me to follow her out the door. Talking to her hens, she slid her hand under their bottoms, stealing eggs. I'd pick through the unoccupied nests collecting the rest. *Buying eggs these days, I have to open the carton, picking through the rows of washed, but often cracked eggs.*

She planted a few rows of tomatoes, okra, string beans, and corn in the garden. "Slice a tomato up and down, not across, so it doesn't get runny. Steam okra quick, so it's not slimy." We'd string beans into a bowl while keeping the ends and strings from falling from our newspapered laps.

There's two ways of cooking green beans. My Granny cooked green beans for hours, cracking the pot lid, adding more water when she put in the potatoes and ham bits. They're dark green and soft, not gray or mushy. The French way, you barely drop them into boiling water before you take them out again; they still crunch.

"You can't mess up cooking ears of corn, but you better not scorch the creamed corn." After she cut off the kernels, scraped the cob clean with her favorite little knife, she added sugar, butter, and milk to the pot while stirring.

Apples, pears, and damsons grew out back. Come late summer, we'd walk into the pasture, scaring away the cows. We'd pick scrappy sour apples off the trees, peel, slice, and cut out rot and worms, then stew apple bits in a big pot on the stove-back until my mouth watered. The aroma filtered out to the front porch. We mashed the cooked apples through the sieve with a wooden pestle. Her fingers knew how much sugar and spice to add before dividing it into square quart plastic containers. She'd pull applesauce out of the freezer the rest of the year for meals or to take to friends. *Now pulling the foil tab off an individualized applesauce serving, I miss Granny's tart sauce.*

She singed the pin feathers off after she plucked a slaughtered chicken, cracking the spine, cleaning out the entrails and slicing the breast. "Your Mama's good at cutting up chickens," she'd say. Like that was worth a lifetime achievement award! *Chicken plucking and cutting up became obsolete within two decades. I don't remember when frozen bits of chicken parts replaced whole birds in the grocery store.*

Granny kneaded bread dough with the heel of her hands then assembled a row of soft mounds. Those buns slapped softly, like a baby's butt when she folded them into baking pans. Sometimes, she gobbed off a bit of dough in each hand. Working magician fingers, she shaped the yeasty pieces for cloverleaf rolls. Her quick moves released perfectly round balls into the muffin tin. She continued until every tin shared three balls. *I taught both daughter and granddaughter to make*

Granny's bread but I can never shape a muffin tin full of smooth identical cloverleaf balls.

Granny sewed when the garden wilted and her daughter took over the housekeeping. Colorful scrap quilts pieced together flower gardens and log cabins, along with memories of play clothes, Easter dresses, Sunday suits, and diminishing hemlines. She needle pointed, handing down that legacy to her daughters and granddaughters. We all sat at her sunlit window painstakingly piercing the webbing with fat needles pulling wool yarns through the mesh.

Granny nurtured African violets, pinching off growth and repotting. The morning light shined on the bowls, saucers and cups filled with velvety blossoms and leaves. The pots covered all the window ledges and shelves of her kitchen and back porch. *I putter in my garden hoping to equal my geraniums and pansies with the ones I remember. I still can't flick a broom.*

Recently my daughter lamented that I never taught her to cook our favorite dishes, to sew or pick out the best vegetables at the market. During her girlhood, I worked. When I had time to show her, she was busy with the marching band. She bypassed home economics class for music and waited tables during summers.

"Mama, how'd you learn to cook and sew?" Daughter never asked, but I thought she might one day.

I endured tedious home economics curriculum, attended artsy-crafty classes, and bought Martha Stewart-type books. I made all my clothes and covered the walls of my home with needlework. "Don't ask me how I know," I'd reply.

PATTY'S LULLABY

It snowed last night covering the tired brown landscape. The geese and birds hunkered down in some warm spot, abandoning the shoreline. Only the dog walkers and step-sweepers venture out. The snow clings to the pine needles and holly hiding the dark branches and scuffle of weeds beneath. Temperatures dropped.

A light breeze stirs the black water. It looks like someone licked the edges of the lake. A foot-wide swath appears where the water blew ashore during the night. Dark trees dressed in white shrouds stand around the edge. White fingers of snow point down to the ground or grasp at the blank sky. A faint smell of a fireplace taunts me as I push my face into the cold. My husband plays his flute. Debussy's haunting Syrinx, keens the death of Pan.

The sun peeks through the clouds and now sapphire waters reflect the sky. Drooping fingers of snow turn icy, like chandeliers in the light. A breeze shifts a branch of pine and snow scatters. It sprays out, a furry pup shaking free of the powder. Spots of evergreen emerge in the light. Icicles drip like sniffling noses onto the porch.

A cocoa mug dollopped by whipped cream tempts me between my stacks of books and papers. I have an assignment to complete and promise myself a reward if I finish before the cup cools. I want to curl up in my grandmother's quilt and watch the snowy wonderland, sipping hot chocolate.

I've sat and watched our lake like a child staring at Saturday morning television.

A lone chickadee braves the snow. He sits on the only spot of the birdfeeder not covered by snow. He's waiting for more sunlight to melt another patch so he can reach the seeds without wetting his feet. More clumps of snow splat below. Not so much from melting, but the wind.

Powdery puffs blow across the road. More sun appears and the snow mocks me. As a child, I donned gloves beneath mittens, cowboy boots, and layers of sweaters beneath the coat to go out and play. The taste of wet wool returns to my mouth like when I teethed-off mittens to free my imprisoned fingers. Sometimes my big sister would run away and hide from me in the snow.

She can't run anymore. My sister lies alone in her king-sized bed. When she gets up to sit by the window in her wheel chair, her head droops on her chest. She loved sitting by the window where she could see the trees turn or snow fall on her mountain. She used to sit on the porch and watch the dogs scrabble along the path chasing rabbits. A disease robbed her of movement and sight.

When she reaches for a glass or a pill, her hand moves more like a paw than the long-fingered hand that drew so beautifully forty years ago. When she worked as a draftsman, her tissue paper drawings were art. Then she became a weaver. Her natural dyed yarns pulled from her own sheep and goats, she spun onto winding arms and wheels paddled by her foot.

The disease snuck in. It started with drop-foot. She thought perhaps it was nerve damage from hauling goats and sheep on the farm. Then it was "a light case of polio" she had as a child. We grew up when newsreels showed children in iron lungs.

Years went by and her shoulders stooped as she climbed her hills. Hands that milked a dozen goats twice daily lost their grasp. After painful bone marrow and blood tests, the cruel verdict was Muscular Dystrophy. She went from cane to walker to wheel chair in less than five years, and then she called me in tears. Her doctor declared her legally blind.

Skilled hospice nurses watched over her while her husband works. I drop into a funk whenever I visit. It's a daylong trip to her mountain. She doesn't want to leave it for a nursing home.

He planned her funeral last week. The doing of the thing, notches that passage irretrievable.

I will stand at her memorial service before a year passes. Her husband covered her casket with mountain flowers and later, we scattered her ashes in her pasture.

It begins to snow again. The sun loses itself in another cloud. My husband feels my mood. Debussy again whines his sorrowful tune towards me.

CHATHAM

We moved to Massachusetts in March. Chatham bloomed like a crocus thrusting aside the crusted snow. The fingers of ice-filled shadows melted in the warming air. The traffic circle blossomed into daffodils, tulips, and cherry trees. Like a starfish, five roads pointed to the business section, the town commons, schools, and out toward gray shouldered, white-trimmed, black-shuttered cottages hunkered into hills and around the water's edge. The stubby lighthouse blinked from the highest point of town. The inlet sucked froth, sea, bits of shell and sand back and forth over hurricane-made sandbars.

Two sentinel windmills stood outside town. The pair of wind sails frozen in position like referees -- feet apart and arms stretched up and out, touchdown! Near the bottom of the hill at Horseshoe Pond, barefoot children hopped among quahog shells and hooded horseshoe crabs, splashing in the still water -- a perfect place to swim without fear of crashing waves.

Two schools at the top of a hill offered clean classrooms, new textbooks, and shining wooden floored gymnasiums. Children respectful of their elders, jumped up from their desks and greeted the principal when he entered, "Good morning Mr. Fishback." Neatly stacked school supplies smelling of paste, crayons and freshly sharpened pencils availed themselves throughout the year.

Local watermen dumped their catch in wire baskets -- lobsters, long-nosed clams, whitefish, and cod. With everyone related or neighbored to a fisherman, fried, boiled, steamed, and baked seafood provided a variety of menu options. Dipped in butter and lemon juice, lobster reigned supreme.

Year-round residents shook out their wares during the summers displaying rental opportunities, antiques, and hand painted art. Streets overflowed with tourists filling shops and restaurants until late fall. Band concerts drew crowds with hampers of food, blankets, and folding lawn chairs. Children pleaded for pinwheels, flags, cotton candy, and ice cream. Fireworks sprayed colorful glitter across the sky to oohs and ahs.

Cicadas and frogs serenaded as attendees walked back to cars or home.

Rose-crowded lattice, like a wedding veil, ran the length of one hotel porch. Flowering window boxes thrived at each building. Two white churches respectfully glared at each other across Main Street. Most of the year, they competed for new members. In the summer, they joined forces selling local strawberries and home-made sponge cake. Tents bloomed on their lawns. Billowing white tablecloths on long tables, covered with dishes of ripe berries mountained by whipped cream, tempted members and guests.

The library stood in the middle of town surrounded by galleries, a local hardware, healthy living stores, and other shops. Filled with books, floor to ceiling, it offered refuge in all seasons against the weather, family, and doldrums of life. The soft-carpeted reference section spun microfilm and caressed thick volumes. Fiction, biography, and children's sections displayed new arrivals to browsers. The smell of leather-bound old and new editions beckoned. Dust motes drifted over bowed heads.

The Epicurean, a three storied establishment, offered wines, liqueurs, crusty breads, flavored coffee beans, cheese, and fruity bottled drinks. Upstairs' renters hung their wash on pulley-lines stretched across the alley -- a veritable cacophony of sights and smells.

Chatham was a quiet town, a gentle town and a giving town to this preadolescent. Crocuses bloom hastily. Their color and fragrance fade too soon. For a few short months, Chatham was my home and then we moved again.

NO LONGER A DAUGHTER

I was fifty when I became a grandmother, fifty-one when my father died. The week before Daddy's death, my head ached with a miserable cold that kept my nose stopped up. My ears popped every time I used the hospital elevator. Like characters in a poorly colorized movie, we trudged through the older hospital into the bright new section of the cardiovascular unit.

"Hello, Daddy! We're here. How ya' doing today? Talk to us," I prompted him. Mamma said little. A friend of the family had already shut her down confiding, "Sarah, you know Sam won't survive this operation.

Very few do." I never spoke to that woman again.

He'd pulled the tubes from his nose and mouth. They tied him down with Velcro straps. Checking his thin ankle and wrist straps to make sure they weren't too tight, I continued to banter. "Mamma's here. Don't you want to talk to her?"

Some days he knew we were there. His eyes and mouth opened and shut, telling stories like a film projector gone wrong. "Did I tell you about being on an icebreaker in the North Atlantic?" Another time, "I saw Abel, Chick, and Smitty last night. They stood right there" — dead men from his past. We listened to his stories, sometimes horrified, sometimes mystified.

He didn't like the black nurse who came to bathe him and change his sheets. "Throw her overboard!" He pointed with a restrained hand and swooshed her washcloth away. No one had bathed him. His wrinkled bedclothes were soiled with body fluids and wear.

"I went for a ride last night. Some of the boys loaned me a car. I drove down the street there." His chin nodded toward the window. A cloudy canister mounted beside his bed forced antiseptic green smoke through tubes into his soggy lungs. I shivered and pulled the blanket up over his chest. Mamma clung to his ice-cold hand, biting her bottom lip.

Other days there was no recognition as we talked to him. Closed eyelids and dehydrated lips moved in his sleep. Dried blood crinkled from his Statue of Liberty nose where a taped tube protruded. A whole week went by and he said nothing more. I called our daughter, "Can you come? I don't think Daddy's going to last much longer."

We met at the hospital. I forced a smile on my face and trooped the family into the room, wheeling Mamma in her chair. "Daddy, that little red-haired girl is here to see you. Remember? It's Rachel, your great granddaughter. You better wake up. She's come all the way from Cary." The strange room and man with tubes frightened the one-year-old. She clung to her father. From a dwindling chamber in my father's mind, he drew strength to break out one last time.

His eyes opened, "Bring her here. Let me see that baby girl," he reached out with bound wrists. "Aren't you something? I see your Mamma over there. Hey, Chris!" The child dangled from her father's arms over Daddy's chest. His hands, bruised by IV needles, gently ran along her head and tugged at her silky dark red hair. "Such a pretty girl." Our hearts applauded his courage struggling out of death's comforting arms. After five minutes, he drifted back behind eternity's curtain.

They called us early the next morning. "He's had a stroke and another heart attack during the night. We misplaced his living will so we've kept him alive for you." Did they really?

New tubes and stimulators invaded my father's body. My mother slumped in her wheelchair holding his jerking hand. We stood around the bed. The doctor assured us the moving arms and huffs were automatic, caused by dying nerves jabbing muscles. "His brain is dead. I'm sorry about the mix-up. I wasn't on duty at the time." A stand-in minister came and prayed with us.

Daddy couldn't feel our touches. He never heard our good-byes. He never told us good-bye either. I used the box of hospital tissues to wipe my runny nose and tears. The stiff, course tissues felt like sandpaper rubbing an already red nose.

A nurse asked us to wheel Mamma down the hall, while she removed the tubes that kept his heart beating and lungs drawing air. When we returned an additional dose of morphine had calmed his flailing arms and quieted his gasps. Veins along his temples and cheeks looked like blue tear-tracks gliding down his face. His body, skin draped over bones, was covered with coarse hospital sheets and a pale blanket -- smoothed by the nurse, in a parting gesture, when she left with her cartful of life-extending equipment.

We watched the monitors. The jumping lines went across the screen. A straight line, then a jag — like our emotions. His once strong heart refused to quit. The line continued to blip, then nothing. We waited. One, two, five minutes.

Walking like zombies down to the hall phone, we called the rest of the family. "Thursday, yes the viewing will be at six. We'll have a graveside service on Friday. Daddy wanted a military burial, flag-draped coffin, and no church fuss. We thought about two o'clock."

My mother raised out of her stupor.
She would join Daddy within a few months.
"What are y'all doing?" She cried at us,
"Planning his funeral? He's not dead yet!"

THINGS I TAUGHT MY GRANDMOTHER

It doesn't take much to make my Grandma happy. The first time, I remember I blew bubbles and smiled at her funny faces. Then I learned to mouth, "Mamaw" and stumble in her direction when she visits. I can't walk good, but my run-stumble gets me there. At this age, if I fall it's not that far to the floor. Now that's the first game I taught her. When I fall, she waits. If I laugh and get up, she cheers but — if I cry, she rushes to pick me up and goo goo's at me.

She doesn't visit that often, so learning my 1,2,3's and A,B,C's came next on my list for her. A while back, just after my third birthday she called me to come look at a magazine. It was a picture of a kid with arms raised, in a bathroom wearing Buz Lightyear Huggy Pull-Ups saying, "Today the potty, tomorrow the universe!" Hmm, I've seen this before.

More than once my parents have propped me over this big seat-hole, called a potty. They say things like, "Let's make pee-pee bubbles" or in a lower voice, "BM!" Usually they run the water in the sink and sit and wait on the stool I use for brushing my teeth. I wait with them. They read me a book, When I Go Potty, which I've heard so often I can recite. If they think I'm "through," we tear off some toilet tissue and drop it into the potty, flush and wash our hands. For some unknown reason, after all that, we raise our hands over our head and shout, "Hurrah!"

Lately the not-as-stressed folks at daycare have been going through the same motions. Hey, I'm a fast learner when not under pressure. I figured out the bathroom door signs. I go in the one with the girl in the dress, even though I don't wear dresses much. If you really want to excite your grandma, take her into the girl's bathroom and touch as much stuff as you can before she stops you. That's always good for a laugh. Ha, ha.

Grandma gave me a couple of months to work on this potty thing before she came back. I learned this new trick at daycare. "Grandma, come watch me," I yell heading for the bathroom, pulling off my pants. I jump on my blue stool and leap-frog onto the potty, like Zorro jumps on his horse, but I face the other way. I lay my book flat on the back of the toilet and not only "read" to her, but also, go potty followed by the routine of tissue wiping, flushing, and hand washing. She is speechless! I get a big hug and then I give her a slobbery kiss, which she loves.

Now I'm working on writing my name and staying between the lines when I color. Hey, like the picture says, "Today the potty, tomorrow the universe!"

MAMA TOLD ME

If you run with scissors or fight with stick swords, you'll put your eyes out. Don't throw the ball up on the roof; you'll ruin the shingles. Look both ways and hold hands crossing the street or you'll get run over. If you don't stop that tussling, someone's gonna get hurt. Share your toys. Keep a clean hanky in your pocket in case your nose runs; don't sit on the toilet seat in a public bathroom. Wash your hands before eating and cover your mouth when you cough. Say Ma'am and Sir when you're talking to adults. Keep your mouth closed while chewing; don't talk with your mouth full. Always say please and thank you. Don't slam the door. Don't wear red; it makes you look fat. Wipe your feet off before you come in the house; hang up your coat in the closet. Don't scratch your privates or pick your nose. Watch out for your little brother. Be nice. Set the table with the fork on the left, the spoon and knife on the right. Watch the hostess; don't put more on your plate than you can eat. Excuse yourself when you get up from the table; take your dishes to the sink when you go. Pick up your dirty clothes and make your bed. Wash your neck and brush your teeth; breathe into your hand to smell if you have bad breath. Wear clean underwear if you're going downtown and be sure there aren't any holes in them. If you're in an accident I don't want them saying you were wearing holey underwear! Keep your hands to yourself; don't mess with your brother; sit on your side of the car and if you're going to be carsick let me know. Unless there's an emergency we aren't stopping on this trip so you better go to the bathroom while you have a chance. Do your homework when you get home, then you can play. No television until after supper. Hang the dishtowels up so they can dry; close the kitchen doors and cupboards if you open them. Date nice boys; always remember you're a lady. Be home by eleven. Here's a dime, call if you need me to come get you. You're too young to get married. You'll never get anywhere if you don't graduate from college. He's not good enough for you. I'll make your wedding dress, but choose your pattern wisely. Empire waistlines make you look thinner. I won't say I told you so. If you're not happy where you are, then move on. I wasn't talking about divorce when I said that. Finish your degree; you can always teach. Do your best; aim high; watch your back. Eat both desserts. Don't do as I do; do what I told you.

I wore a red dress to my second wedding. I still have that dress and that husband. I asked my daughter what advice I gave her.

She said, "Nothing's fair in life, don't wipe your nose on your elbow and don't swing on the refrigerator door."

BOATING BLUES, GREENS, AND PURPLES

If you had told me twenty years ago I would give up a good paying job, a two bathroom, three bedroom house with landscaped yard, and walk-in closets loaded with "power suits" to live aboard a boat offering living space no bigger than an average master bath, questionable plumbing, unknown income, unscheduled days -- but with a waterfront view, I'd have laughed in your face. My pocket calendar displayed hourly sessions with clients and important meetings. I was a deacon in the church. My aging parents lived next door and — I was a grandmother. I couldn't live on a boat.

During extended weekend cruises, I busied myself scouring the stainless steel stanchions, waxing the cockpit or concocting a novel lunch treat while my husband relaxed, navigated, enjoyed the scenery. He often beckoned me to stop and sit with him. A former live-aboarder, he was glad I'd acquiesced and taken off from work to enjoy an occasional cruise. It was the least I could do. My father built both our family boats and I was a Girl Scout! I could rough it with the best of 'em.

It was only after my husband cajoled me into sneaking off for an entire month that I latched onto the idea of full-time boat living. During that month of freedom, we enjoyed the rivers and sounds of North Carolina, headed north to the Chesapeake Bay or south to Charleston.

During the first years of our monthly trips, it took me a week to relax, care less about the following day's passage, and not worry about our next meal. Did you know marsh grass grows in seven shades of green?

Each spring we either inhaled salty breezes of North Carolina, spicy seasonings from Chesapeake waterside restaurants, musky marshes of Georgia or ligustrum fragrance along South Carolina's waterways. I became a Martha Stewart one-pot cook. Meals morphed from preparation headaches into fun conversations with new boating friends and old acquaintances. Tea and cereal motivated us to weigh anchor and glide past sleepy communities. Office multi-tasking habits were lost, as well as manicured nails and permed coif. I could change oil or fuel filters and splice dock lines as well as my partner.

After five years of our monthly sojourns, we made the commitment to break away and work toward living aboard. Major boat preparations for comfort and safety were completed. Financial sacrifices included getting rid of the second car, reducing expenses and living on one retirement pension. We set up bank drafts, direct deposits, and account ledgers. I procured a mail forwarding service, e-mail device, and cellular phone. I packed up, gave away or yard-saled clothes, housewares, family heirlooms, wedding gifts, and furniture we couldn't store. To this day, I regret some of those heartless decisions.

My husband packed a couple of jeans, a handful of shorts, t-shirts, and a nice pair of slacks and collared shirt for special occasions. This woman needed cool, versatile, easily-washed clothes as well as grubbies for boat work. I packed my "nice clothes" in zip-locked bags and slid them under the settee to ride wrinkle-free on top of the water tank. I gleaned my foot wardrobe down to walking shoes, sandals, and shower clogs.

Some live-aboarders have refrigerator-freezers, washer/dryer combinations and all their house accoutrements. If we were going to make the break, we had to confront our austerity issues! Our sailboat, a 32' Bayfield, and later, the 27' Alban trawler had little free space. They say, "The smaller the boat the greater the adventure." We worked through our storage frustrations.

When my retirement was approved, we had six months to prepare the boat and ourselves. We browsed boat stores, hardware centers, marinas, and boatyards like hungry scavengers. I bought a cheap sewing machine for canvas repairs and clothes mending. We studied charts, navigational equipment, and talked with other full-time boaters. We learned T'ai Chi to keep agile, practiced giving one another haircuts, earned concealed weapon permits, and attended boat fests. I wrote my first paying article for a boating magazine.

We rented the house, moved aboard in May, and prepared for North Carolina's hurricane season. That fall we headed south for the winter. In the following years, we journeyed from Baltimore to the Florida Keys. We listened to Boston Pops perform their Fourth of July Concert, complete with caissons in Vero Beach. Waterspouts and micro-bursts descended with a fury that left us drinking up rainbows. We witnessed the Cassina as well as other space launches, boat parades showing off twelve months of computer engineering, watched high-rise bridges replace draw bridges, and laughed or admired every ilk of waterfront sculpture and residence. We've watched birds, manatee, fish, raccoon, deer, alligators, and snakes cross our bow. Rude boaters, like their highway counterparts, victimized us. One night I was so afraid at one anchorage, I slept with the gun.

A new vocabulary emerged with living aboard. Did you know that ropes on board are lines? Lines hold you to the dock; lines keep you away from the dock. Lifeline, halyard, rode, mooring, shroud, sheet and painter were a few of my daily lines. Lines wore through canvas, rubbed against the bowsprit, and slapped against the mast at night creating a lulling concert for sleep. Lines ripped from hands in a gale and held dancing clothes when we cruised on wash day. I banged my ankles black and blue on winches as I scurried about the cockpit. When we sold the sailboat in favor of a small trawler, I told myself, "No more line-dancing!" I was wrong. Lines still connected us to dock, dinghy, and the Danforth anchor.

Miami waters are teal blue, the Albemarle Sound turns navy blue with an approaching storm, and Carolina blue skies watched over most of our journeys. Away from city lights, shooting stars zoomed overhead nightly. Ebony skies domed quiet anchorages. I counted neighbors by their anchor lights swaying in the night. A cacophony of frogs, crickets, marsh hens, night herons, and sloshing sounds of some small animal serenaded us. Shrimp scratched, manatee moaned, and puppy drum hum-thrummed beneath our hull. Ospreys screamed if we ventured too close. Pelicans tiptoed on wingtips across the water and porpoises discoed in our bow waves. Most mornings, orange skies punctuated with a beach ball sun chased away the last star. Purple clouds climbed above the horizon.

Along with the joy of new sights, sounds, and smells enjoyed living aboard, a miracle of "partnership" bloomed. For us, a full-fledged symbiosis developed. We'd sit a few feet from one another and be miles apart mentally or be separated by the length of the boat and knew what the other was thinking.

I've seen boaters alienate their spouses, as well as other travelers. They set anchor, jump in the dinghy and zip over to visit. If two people can't sit quietly by themselves relaxing their minds and bodies after a hard crossing, they don't need to share their despair with another couple. Forget "marriage encounter weekends." If you want to rejuvenate a relationship, go off for a month-long boat trip, together.

We've discovered small coastal towns, made life-long friends, collected unforgettable memories, and shared extreme moments of fear. We've endured El Nino winters on the west coast of Florida, Lake Okeechobee droughts and endless nights of bouncing, hull-slapping anchorages. We've stayed at delightful quirky marinas, anchored in quiet gunk holes, borrowed marina "loaner cars" that wouldn't make it through the NC inspection stations and laughed more than God allows -- at others and ourselves.

When the boat seemed like more work than fun, we decided to sell. Our boat/home sold sight unseen while we docked in Marathon, Florida. The buyer wanted us to bring it back to North Carolina. We did.

Our traveling days now are in a hybrid car. She gets over 50 miles to a gallon. That beats the boat ten times over. The car is smaller but a lot faster than the boat. A day's journey by boat is an hour by car. We travel now without wind, sun, and rain in our faces. Before, no matter where we tied up we were home — with all our belongings. Now, we carry luggage from car to room at night. I miss the journey but not the boat. Car traveling, we notice little oddities that still make us laugh. Like the other day, I noticed our car's reversed trademark — backwards through the windshield it read, "A TOY(Y)OT."

Originally written for The Rambler Magazine.

THE STRING QUARTET: A CONCERT

They come early to see the show. Gray heads, peering over Buick steering wheels, parade caravan-style through the parking lot in search of handicapped spaces. Brake lights declare stops at the front door to allow a walker, cane, or wheelchair to emerge pursued by stooped, beaded, sweatered or thin-haired seniors. Faces smile, hands shake, embraces of gold glittered shells with delicate wraps falling from thin shoulders, suits pulled from mothballs and shaken, smoothed by wrinkled hands, "It's alright, honey. It'll do just fine."

A potpourri of cologne mingles with cigarette smoke in the narrow entrance. Inside, tweeds mix with silk, golf shirts and plaid slacks, wing tips and sandals. Botoxed faces, eyebrows penciled over shimmering lids, cheeks cloaked with rouge, blush with excitement. Dandruff flakes fall on dark shoulders, fishnet shawls over jersey, swirling rayons dust the floor. "This string quartet concert performs once a year."

Instruments tuning, four-cocktail slurring, laughter tinkling, prissy heels clicking on linoleum, colliding canes and walkers, cigarette-coughing and a toilet flushing in the restroom down the hall. "Hello, so nice to see you." "It's a lovely evening." "So glad you could come." "Do you have your tickets?"

Lights blink; conversation fades to whisper. Eyes study the program. A polite clapping beckons the quartet. They bow, clutching their instruments like children lost in a hug. Three men in tuxedos with open collars and French cuffs, and a young Japanese woman in a pink ruffle-necked frock mount the stage. But wait. "Did you see that? When she bows, you can see -- everything beneath her ruffles." She bows repeatedly, like the Japanese do. There's an urge to grab her shoulders and hold her upright.

Smiling, they squat to teeter on chair edges, one foot in front, instruments whispering in their ears, bows raised, eyes alert for some silent count; they caress their strings. The minuet, then sonata stream across the dark auditorium silencing the last gossipers. The quartet weaves like wheat in the wind to gypsy, bee-bop, and passion. The cellist saws his strings, concentrating eyes downward, he swoons with his bow. The male violinist dips and nods, eyes shut in fervor. The violist smiles, for he sits across from the Japanese violinist who plunges low to lower and exposes her lacy pink bra over tiny breasts. Hayden's music echoes from one side to another and she smiles, her painted lips with porcelain skin and black hair move in their own performance.

In mock delight, never knowing her body bends from her waist -- downward, elbows almost touching the floor, she emotes with her bow and fiddle. Her tongue peeks out of cherry lips. She concentrates. Ridges mar her forehead as she plays, one woman on a stage with three men. The violist beams as he sweeps his head and shoulders in tune, for he enjoys his view as does the audience seated left of center stage.

A guest English horn player enters, with cropped hair and cheeks that fill out like the clown blowing up balloons at a birthday party. Puffs of air squash through her reed as she duels with the string instruments. She sits priggishly in her satin tuxedo in contrast to pink ruffles. English horn's prim feet together, she barely moves with her instrument to sounds of Americana, streets of bustling people, cars and trains. Intermission and music connoisseurs clap while leaning forward to rise, as the performers file out -- after another series of bows, dips, and revelations.

More hugs and shoulder tapping, "How marvelous, don't you think?" Like the emperor's new clothes, no mention of the ruffles expose'. Makeup wilts in lobby lights, hands chase invisible lint from laps and husbands jingle pocket change. They'd rather be home watching the game. Icy metallic-tasting water dribbles down chins at the water fountain. Preening begins in the ladies' room. Some white heads begin to droop with the late hour, retired musicians of bygone concerts. The audience files back to their seats like kindergarteners. Some bend to retrieve the program from the floor. If not, the janitor will sweep it up tomorrow.

The narration reads, "An energetic, elegant interpretation, fiery and amusing skirmishes." The lights blink again and Brahms invites an alto clarinet to banter with the strings. The final selection is a battle of counterpoint chitchat among the woodwind and strings, while the Japanese woman continues to sweep the floor with her sleeve.

Encore! The audience rises, exhausted, as if they physically ran with the notes rather than listening. Another encore, flower bouquets, and expressions of thanks follow. Eyes search for the woman in pink. She's gone, lost in the clutch of admirers who rush to shake hands and congratulate. Searching for the car in the darkness, some commit to memory the concert music, as others remember the woman wearing pink ruffles on porcelain skin.

A PANTOUM: THE ANCHORAGE

We swing on anchor at slack tide
near the marsh at river's edge
Squawking birds divvy a fish
Fiddler crabs scuttle over pocked mud

Near the marsh at river's edge
we listen to wetlands crackling with life
Fiddler crabs scuttle over pocked mud
Pelicans glide on fingertips

We listen to wetlands crackling with life
as marsh hens wade along the shore
Pelicans glide on fingertips
Gulls stand guard on barnacled roosts

As marsh hens wade along the shore

shrimp scratch beneath our keel
Gulls stand guard on barnacled roosts
The ooze bestows a heady scent

Shrimp scratch beneath our keel
Dolphins snort, playing tag
The ooze bestows a heady scent
A breeze ripples the air

Dolphins snort, playing tag
Small creatures croak in the ebbing light
A breeze ripples the air
as stars rise on the falling tide

Small creatures croak in the ebbing light
Sunlight smears crimson across the sky
As stars rise on the falling tide
A dog barks in the distance

Sunlight smears crimson across the sky
Dawn tip-toes to paint golden reeds
A dog barks in the distance
Egrets soar in the gilded light

Dawn tip-toes to paint golden reeds
Squawking birds divvy a fish
Egrets soar in the gilded light
We swing on anchor at slack tide

VELVETEEN STOCKINGS

The evergreens hang on the door. The cranberry pie weeps berry juice and walnuts through the crust. Ambrosia chills in the refrigerator. Wrapped presents hide under the bed. Christmas music plays all day. But, Christmas isn't here until our beaded, sequined, satin-lined velveteen stockings dangle from the mantel. I was five years old when Granny stitched the first stockings. She continued stocking-making not only for all of the 28 grandchildren, but also her eight children and their spouses.

Granny's apron pockets bulged with tiny silver scissors, thimble, cardboard patterns, spools of thread, and scraps of velveteen. Sitting by the window in the den, she stitched pearls, colored beads, and glistening sequins spelling out our names, outlining miniature hearts, candles -- Christmas silhouettes and family symbols.

On Christmas morning, I'd creep down the creaking stairs carrying a flashlight. In our family with four children, two parents, an aunt and grandmother, Santa Claus identified each gift pile with our velveteen stockings. I had no problem finding my own, peeking at all Santa brought, warned beforehand by Mama not to open a wrapped gift. I grabbed my stocking first.

It bulged. My pudgy fingers felt the treasures inside the slick lining. "I got nuts, an orange, gold-wrapped chocolate coins, #2 pencils with my name printed on them, and a chocolate marshmallow Santa!"

"Shh, be quiet. You'll wake up Mama and Daddy," my big sister scolded, looking at her paints, frilly socks, charm bracelet, and fruit. I chose one toy to carry back up to bed.

Just when Granny was ready to hang up her tiny silver velveteen stocking scissors, we older girls began marrying. She set to work stitching velveteen log cabin wedding quilts. My quilt is made of rose, aquamarine, and gray "logs." My sister's is navy, gold, and pale blue. I store mine in Mama's cedar chest, when it's not lying across the top of our couch in the winter months. I have no passion for stitching log cabin velveteen quilts.

I made velveteen stockings for my husband, and my daughter and helped cut out velveteen shapes for my grandchildren. My husband's stocking has a boat. My daughter's has a heart. Her Great Granny's handmade tatting borders her name. When my grandson was born four days before Christmas, my daughter and I hurriedly sewed together his stocking. We used some of the pieces from Mama and Daddy's stockings, which were tucked away after they died.

Over the years Christmas ornaments broke, were lost or given away. A tree with lights pre-strung "in three pieces for easy assembly," replaced our cedar tree. But, every time we moved, living on the boat or on land, the velveteen stockings were there.

They hung by the mantel or the mast, surrounded by family or with just my husband. The stockings proclaimed Christmas.

I'll give my daughter and granddaughter my wedding quilt one day. I don't think they'll carry on the quilting tradition. However, I have beads, sequins, and a string of tiny pearls in my sewing basket. The next time my granddaughter comes, I'll teach her how to make bead and sequined velveteen stockings.

DOWNSIZING BY PRIORITY

I was working at my desk when the phone rang. I answered it mechanically, still reading my computer screen. "Mrs. Dodd, this is Doctor Franks. I have the results of your procedure." It was my first colonoscopy. We were going on a seven-month cruise on our boat. I decided to go ahead and have it done before the trip.

He said, "You have cancer." His quiet voice set off alarms in my brain.

Not hearing the rest, I grabbed a pen, scrawled large capital letters, "CANCER" on a scrap of paper, and passed it across to my husband who was playing Minesweeper on his laptop computer. He stood and stumbled around to my side. "Who, our daughter? The grandkids?" My husband's voice doubled over the doctor's.

My hand reached to the side of my desk for the colored shots of bowel that lay in the heap of unfiled receipts, bills, and deposit slips. We had joked about the pictures, "Shall we put them in the family album or have them framed and hung over the mantel?" My ear ached with the pressure of the receiver against my head.

"Carcinoma," he repeated.

I remembered the doctor, dressed in golf shirt, khaki slacks, and tasseled loafers, striding jauntily into the hospital procedure room. The doctor looked so young; maybe he should have been bouncing a basketball and wearing high-top sneakers. He held up a James Taylor tape, asking for my approval. "Any questions before we begin?" He slid the cassette into the boom box while a nurse adjusted my IV. I slid under to the sound of Baby James.

"Can you say again what you just told me?" My analytical brain kicked in. "I want to write this down." Word for word, he patiently spelled out the verdict, describing the polyp the pathologist examined. "If you were my," he paused, "sister, I'd recommend immediate surgery." He could have said Mother. "Would you like me to call and make an appointment with a surgeon?" My young Dr. Franks was polite, trying hard to maintain his professional role by phone, while listening to my sobs.

We downsized when I retired to move onto our boat. We got rid of things, responsibilities, ties to the community and acquaintances. My husband and I formed "a more perfect union" blending into one distinct spirit while cruising. We could sit a few feet apart for hours and be in separate worlds, yet know when the other had an itch. Our union irreversibly spliced into a world of water and boat.

The joy of retirement snuffed out. Later that night, I sat on the edge of our bed and cried into handfuls of tissue. Would I live to see my grandchildren graduate? Would I have a painful death? How would my husband survive a second wife's death? Could he find his way among all my carefully filed boxes of taxes and important papers?

In the months between that first phone call and surgeon's final release, we downsized once again. Neighborhood squabbles, international politics, violent books, and gory movies were eliminated from our sphere. Our time slowed like the syrupy days we had spent on the Waccamaw River, drifting in the currents. My husband and I found ourselves touching and listening to one another as if it were our last conversation.

Annual colonoscopies continue to remind me of that thin film that separates us from death. I hold my breath each year until the report comes. I find myself encouraging strangers to have the procedure. Life changes with a phone call. While researching defensive cancer living, I discovered something Gilda Radner wrote. She said that cancer helps us set priorities. If it weren't for the downside, everybody would want to have it.

SHORT STORIES

MUD ANGEL

Kate, lying flat on her back with rain thumping her face, carefully sucked in air. The bullet had passed beneath her ribs; she'd bleed out if someone didn't find her soon. She tried to roll over, but the pain in her back jabbed like a branding iron. Way to go, Kate, you've done it good this time. Licking the rain from her lips, she thought about her life as rain soaked into the prairie.

When she was young and agile, she liked working outdoors. Herding cattle appealed to her. The pay, working with animals and her own private thoughts kept her where she wanted to be. After the chores each night, she'd pull out a book from her saddlebag and read until dark.

She found a man who'd put up with her shameless habits. She'd gone into one of those sit and sip bookstores to buy a winter's supply of paperbacks. He'd gone into the store following her, because he liked the way she filled out a pair of jeans. Tom stepped in front of her when she turned in the aisle. "How long does it take you to read all those books?"

Their cowboy boots pointed at each other while she studied his gray eyes. Liking what she saw, Kate cocked her head.

"Do you always cut and tag your heifers in bookstores?"

He handed her a book she'd dropped and smirked, "Better than bar roundups and I always find a lady who, at least, knows how to read."

Working their ranch, they often curled spoon-like in sleeping bags, counting the stars. As partners, they raised the ranch and two sons; she kept a pile of her unread books by her nightstand. Kate still rode the last drive each spring and she kept a paperback in her saddlebag. He kidded her about her soft-covered novels. She called him her bookstore cowboy.

When moving cattle these days, the family found that weather controlled the schedule. They rarely lost any stock to thieves. Occasionally one of the Indians from the reservation would cut out a steer and butcher it. Tom had said, "Let it go. They were here first, I reckon."

The cattle thieves of yesteryear progressed; their computers scheduled butchering and sales before they stole the herd. These days, rustlers came with 18-wheelers and ramps driving their booty along hardtop roads into the night.

The family camped near the highway where water, a patch of grass, and a gate allowed them to move across the road in the morning. The purple sky rumbled as they watched a storm approach. A few trucks swished by in the early evening rain. The herd huddled together moaning when the storm finally broke. Kate, Tom, and their sons slept in their clothes and tethered their horses under a lean-to near the camper.

Rustlers attacked at the peak of the storm on three-wheelers and motorbikes. The family jumped up and tugged on their boots as the cattle broke their knot of brown bodies to run wide-eyed. Kate handed out rifles and handguns to the men in their creaking saddles. A loud ping, a bullet ricocheted off the tire rim as she pulled herself up on her own swirling horse.

The mare bolted under her and Kate held the reins in her mouth, urging the horse with subtle movements of her legs. Her fingers wrapped around her gun. She lined up her sights but her shot passed through empty air. When a rustler fired in return, she lost her balance in the saddle.

Kate fell from her horse a half-mile from their camp. Could they find her in the darkness? Chagrined she listened to body whispers and a grazing horse. The aches from the fall hurt worse than the bullet wound.

She turned her head in the direction of the road. Her fading blonde hair mixed with the mud and pebbles. In the distance, she heard vehicles and felt vibrations of hooves. The muck beneath her cheeks smelled of cow dung and fresh rain. If she could fire her gun, they might find her in time. Kate painfully moved her arms up and down making mud angels while her fingers felt for the gun. When the searching hand finally gripped the pistol, she drifted, riding her favorite mare -- with a paperback tucked in her saddlebag. The storm had passed and the sky was stoking up to be a beautiful day.

STAR STRUCK

The only thing more frightening than having a seasick person on board a boat was having a seasick person on board, holding a gun. The boat started rocking as the storm approached. My assassin-to-be started yawning and turning green shortly thereafter. The hull banging against fender, fender against dock, closed quarters, and pounding rain added to his misery. Clamped jaw and clutched fist caused my neck and shoulders to spasm. I thought back to how this all started.

The day I found my realtor husband diddling a new home buyer, I pulled the plug on our marriage. We drew straws on the pets, the house, and the boat. Vinnie gave away the dog and sold our bungalow to move in with Ladonna. She calls him Vincent.

I live on the sailboat, Aldeberan, with a cat. I'm a school teacher. Mama named me Vega — for the star not the car, because she has this thing for constellations and it carries over to me and boat names.

"Darn it." Emily Goins, my middle school teaching partner says, "I can't get on-line for my account balances. These totals aren't right. Have you ever looked at your retirement accounts online?"

I shrug. "This close to retirement I'm socking everything into Treasuries. Why don't you call that investment advisor, what's his name?" His emery board calling card sticks out of my Rolodex. I Frisbee it to her.

"He never gave me one of these." She picks up the phone, dials, and leaves a message after listening to a recording. "Mr. Demsey, this is Emily Goins. Can you call me back?"

Emily comes around her desk, "Look, this report I got last month says I have close to $54,000 and the printout I got off the screen says only $14,000." We have team-taught for ten years. By now, I'm used to her meticulousness. "I have no idea. You sure ya' put in the right account numbers?"

She nods emphatically, "Yes, I did." and goes back to her tidy desk. Her grades post before mine. All her sharpened pencils point in the same direction and her side of our office looks like a school supply catalog picture.

Mine, on the other hand, is a war zone. Folders dumped inside milk crates with sharp things, like scissors, sticking out the bottom. My purse and a high-top tennis shoe that I can't explain rest against the wall.

Twenty years ago, school higher-ups thought team-teaching was the way to go. Emily and I divvy up classroom responsibilities. I teach language arts and social studies. She focuses on math and science. Now they talk about self-contained classrooms for next year. I'll leave that thought on my desk when I leave for the summer.

I count the days until vacation and flick my calendar shut. When school lets out, I slip dock lines from my berth to head south for summer breezes, and solitude, single-handing my boat to points unknown.

"My grades are in the computer waiting for your tallies," she says. Grabbing her monogrammed handbag, she applies a fresh coat of Ripe Lush Gloss and exits to the teachers' workroom where her betrothed awaits.

Ivan Montgomery popped the question last Christmas. He's not a bad guy for an attorney. Emily's made a humongous wedding notebook and shared it with me. I have no interest since my former husband, Vinnie, started his shenanigans about the same time.

"Miz Connelly?" One of our favorite students, Jeremy, peers in the office from behind mega-lensed glasses. "We're working on our project and want to know if we can sorta turn the classroom into a real restaurant." Manuel politely waits behind him. Manuel wears clean hand-me-down clothes. Having taught in the same school for over twenty years, I know all the multi-child families.

The assignment is to develop a financial plan, equipment, and supply lists, menu, staffing, and interior design for an eatery. Usually I get a pizza parlor scratched out on lined notebook paper and magazine cutouts pasted on poster board.

"Sure." I give them my best teacher smile. "Just remember to put it back in order before we leave for the weekend." After posting grades, I shut down the computer, toss more folders in the bin, clean off the desk top, and remind myself only two more years before retirement!

Arriving home, I note the diver's come and gone. This morning the boat's bottom growth looked like dread-locks. This afternoon, a clean waterline smiles back. I slide open the companionway hatch. Two-Ton, my long-haired calico cat, crawls out from under the v-berth and stretches. Potty training her was a top priority when I moved aboard. Always helpful, Emily found a magazine article about the technique. Two-Ton took the hint. I note with delight she's used the head and not left little surprises for me in the galley. "Good kitty! Here's a treat." She blinks and continues washing her paws. I shed my teacher clothes and shower in the tiny bathroom. Living on board, I can brush my teeth, shower, and pee at the same time — handy when I oversleep.

Starting and running the engine for an hour is a Friday afternoon chore. As the boat thrums away, I tote my laundry down the dock to the laundry room and set the timer on my watch. In thirty minutes, I'll be back to shift the wash to the dryer.

The lid on my Mama's iron skillet rattles on top of leftover roast, carrots, and little potatoes. She reminded me to bring the skillet back when I finished re-heating her Sunday dinner. I usually get it back with another plastic container of frozen leftovers. With the companionway open, I smell my supper halfway down the dock. Reheating frozen leftovers is how I like to end a week.

Saturday morning I'm supposed to meet Emily for a yard sale marathon. It puts a cramp in my finishing the weekend chores, but what are friends for? I wait patiently in her driveway. After twenty minutes, I call her on my cell phone. She doesn't answer. Maybe Ivan stayed over and she got a late start. I certainly don't want to see any lovemaking between a gung-ho teacher and a milk-toast attorney. Ringing the bell, I peer in the window by the front door - ok, I do want to see.

Emily's townhouse is an end unit. I walk to the back and climb on a garbage can to look in the kitchen window. I wish I hadn't. "Emily?" Long limbs askew, blond hair trapped in a pool of blood, she sprawls face up. Minutes pass until the window coolness against my cheek pulls me from my stupor. I run to the car and dial 911 while digging in my purse to find the key she gave me a while back.

Her once pristine home looks tossed like a surreal television scene. Shards of glass, food, and paper litter the floor from kitchen to front door, her wedding notebook pulled apart, the engagement photograph torn in half. I step around the glass and blood. Have only minutes passed since I peered in?

Chills shake my body. She's gone, but I try anyway. "Honey, can you hear me?" My ears whisper back like a conch shell, my face numbs, and my body goes into automatic mode. I don't remember hitting the answering machine button when I back into the kitchen cabinets.

The machine rewinds, "Emily, this is Vinnie Connelly. About the house, I'm sure we can work something out. Don't tell anyone about, ah, our little problem. I got a lot riding on this. You understand? Gimme a call, please." A sharp beep ends the message. What has Vinnie got to do with this?

"Pardon me, but who are you?" A plain clothes policeman flashes his badge. I nearly jump out of my skin. Crepe-soled shoes silenced his arrival. My head feels like a giant vacuum just sucked everything out. My knees buckle at the combination of Vinnie's voice within sight of my teaching partner's body.

I come to on the couch. The police detective's ice blue eyes haven't blinked since I opened mine. "I'm Thomas Wyles, investigating officer. You feeling better?" he hands me a glass of water.

"I feel like a dope. I don't usually pass out, but I don't usually find a body."

"Tell me about it," he suggests. "Who you are? Why you're here? How you got in?"

Taking a deep breath, I explain about our yard sale date. Other people pass by as we talk. "She gave me her house key," I open my palm showing the key. It dug a red mark into my hand. He explains to me about the seriousness of disturbing a crime scene.

I bristle, "You wanted me to stay outside? What if she was still alive? Maybe I could have done something."

"Maybe you could have gotten yourself killed. What if who ever did this was still in the house?" he counters.

My morning bagel flip-flops in my stomach. A wave of nausea strikes. One hand on my stomach, the other on my head, I say, "I'll be ok. Let me lie here while you ask your questions."

It's noon before he finishes gathering information from me about Emily. Did Ivan or Vinnie kill Emily? I play both scenarios in my mind as I climb into my Hybrid and drive back to the marina. Two-Ton senses all's not right with the world and drops her haughtiness. The cat climbs up, letting me rub her head while she kneads my lap. Emily gave me the towel rack for the galley. I mope, thinking about the good times we shared. Her energy and encouragement beam out at me from our past.

Activity will help my mood. Fighting grief, I pull on cut-offs and grab the bucket, brush, and hose for a serious deck wash down.

By mid-afternoon, I've worked up a sweat and I'm hungry. I rinse off the last bit of soap and coil the hose. Investigating Officer Wyles, dressed in suit and crepe-soled shoes, heads my way. "Good afternoon," I say. "Did you catch him already?"

"What makes you think it's a 'he'?" I give him a blank stare. "No. I've got more questions." Motioning him out of the sun, I grab an old towel to wipe the cockpit dry. He inspects my boat with a mild curiosity. "Sweet. How long have you had her? How do you like living aboard?" He talks in strings of questions.

"We owned her five years, but I moved on board over Christmas holidays." I pause while he looks at me. "I've got some soda in the 'frig. Want one?" My humble abode has all the modern conveniences; they're just smaller. "I like it here. No grass to cut, no high utility bills, no neighborhood one-up-man-ship, and a waterfront view!" I hand him a can through the companionway and follow. "You didn't come here to ask me about my boat. What's up?"

He draws a notebook out of his jacket pocket. "Tell me about your ex-husband."

"Vinnie and I go back to high school. He's cocky, slick, a slime ball, but I thought I loved him. Emily and Ivan were using him as a realtor to find a new place. She asked me if I minded. I didn't."

"What about Ivan? Have you ever seen him angry?"

"Ivan's a wuss, a real pussy cat as far as I know. He deals in real estate and family law, not a criminal lawyer type. Emily is, er was, the driving force in that relationship."

"Do you think either man's capable of murder?"

"No."

"Any problems you've noticed between the victim and either man?" He probes.

"I don't know about problems!" Wyles considers my words. His eyes match the blue stripe in his tie.

"Do you know about Sable Estates, the new property on the Sound?"

"Naw," I drain the Coke can and toss it into a bucket. "Emily and Ivan liked it and put money down, pending the survey." He writes something in his little book.

The Coke wasn't enough. "I'm starved," I say. "You want something?" The dockside Marina Café by late afternoon belches out hot grease and Cajun spices. I stand up to get my money. He looks like he may join me.

"No. How about a rain check?" Detective Wyles steps back on the dock and leaves. His aftershave lingers. I'd like to fan it below to mask the mildew. Reaching in my purse, I find money and my cell phone. After punching in the numbers, I hear Vinnie's new wife answer.

"Ladonna, is Vinnie there?"

"No, what do you want?" She's Miss Congeniality today. "Vincent had to go out."

"Tell him I called. I want to know what the deal is between him and Emily Goins." I hang up before she can ask why.

The cheeseburger's perfect. The meat hangs down outside the seeded bun, over lettuce, tomato, dill strips in a sloppy ooze of ketchup and mayonnaise. Licking the last off my fingers, I see Vinnie walking out toward the boat. It's not the first time he's ruined my appetite.

I follow grudgingly. When I find him on board, Two-Ton's nestled in his lap. Traitor.

"Hey, Vinnie, what's with you and Emily? I heard your answering machine message." I jump in the cockpit and pretend to care about what he says.

"Vega, baby, I'm in a jam here. You gotta help me. Police crawling all over my office! They think I killed your teaching buddy." He's changed his cologne since the last time I cared. His clothes come from a higher priced rack and his hair's styled.

"Why ask me? You have someone else helping you these days." Reaching over, I take the cat and notice cat hair all over his tailored slacks.

"Yeah, but they think we, Emily and I, had a, what you call, a confrontation. It didn't go that way — just a little problem. I went over there to try to talk her down a bit. Water tests came back with something having too high a reading! I was getting it resolved. Told her not to worry. The woman went ballistic. She's been talking to other buyers, like it's a crime to offer a house with bad water. How was I to know? Christ, it's the first I heard about it. I didn't kill her. She was alive when I left." He runs his skinny fingers through his hair, mussing the mousse. "If word gets out Sable Estates is un-saleable, I'm busted! I can't have that, all over a frigging well."

"I can't help you, Vinnie." Behind me, I hear the distinct tap of high heels on dock planks. She's stepping carefully so she won't break her heels or her scrawny neck. I don't turn around.

"Vincent, how much longer are you going to be? We need to go, sweetie. Now." He seems to genuflect as he climbs to the dock. His Catholic Irish-Italian genes go deep.

"You believe me, don't you?" He tries once more to gain my support. "Vega, you finish every crossword puzzle you start. Finding Emily's killer should be easy for you." He taps his temple, "I never had any complaints about your mind, Baby."

"Vincent!" Ladonna stamps her tiny feet and pulls him away.

Vinnie's remark stings. I chew on my lip, watching them walk down the dock. Now how am I supposed to react to that?

Cat in lap, I lean my head back on the cabin bulkhead to consider possible killers.

Could Ivan be "the terrible?" Had I ever seen any unexplained bruises on Emily from his abuse? Was there a side of him I never knew? I try to see him shooting her in a fit of rage but the picture never develops. Vinnie's the one who always blew a fuse. I nap with dreams of Ivan and Vinnie twirling above her bloody body until my phone rings.

"Vega? It's Sam Harris." He's the school principal and he's heard the news. "There's only a couple more weeks of school. How do you feel about going it alone? You've handled the classes all year. Putting a substitute in there will do more harm than good, don't you agree?" Sam's a good administrator. He's right. The last two weeks of school are little more than babysitting.

"Do I have a choice? How 'bout you take away my lunchroom duty and excuse me from the end-of-year county meeting to give me time to get everything finished and we have a deal," I counter.

He grumbles, but I'm a good teacher. "Done deal. You always know how to handle this ol' man." He's saved some money and

I'm relieved of a few teacher aggravations. I do a little victory dance.

On Monday, students are curious and quiet. Before leaving for the day Manuel reminds me they'll be setting up their student restaurant on Friday.

I've been procrastinating about cleaning out Emily's things. The police aren't interested in her desk drawers of teaching stuff so I empty them. All that's left of Emily is a box of books, makeup, and a handful of change. Folding the sweater she kept hanging on the back of her chair, I can smell her scent. Her investment reports are stacked on her desk corner. She changed the beneficiary to Ivan. Did he know? Is money the motive? Maybe I should call Detective Wyles.

Emily left Richard Demsey's card sticking out of my Rolodex. Another question pops in my mind so I dial the number. His secretary picks up. "This is Vega Connelly. I'm trying to reach Mr. Demsey, regarding Emily Goins. Would you tell him I called?"

The rest of the week goes smoothly until Friday. On entering my classroom after break, I discover the best little Mexican restaurant in town. Burritos, salsa, and tortilla smells fill the room. A costumed student seats me at a table covered with bowls of tempting appetizers. Manuel's mother commandeers the cooking area. His father strums a guitar. Sam, my principal, enters, following his nose and the sound of the Mariachi band. Other invited staff members show up. Jeremy seats Sam and the school secretary at my table. Sombreros, serapes, and colorful banners hang on the walls. Emily would be so proud.

We spend the rest of the day enjoying the music and food. By late afternoon, our restored room bears a whiff of Mexican food and a few crushed chips on the rug. I go home with one of those rare teacher highs, glowing.

There's a knock on the hull as I pull on my boat clothes. A face I vaguely remember says, "Mrs. Connelly, I'm Dick Demsey."

"Ah, Emily's investment advisor. You didn't have to come down, but since you're here, come aboard."

He hesitates before placing a wing-tipped shoe on board, but I reach and help him step over. “Thank you. You know client confidentiality keeps me from sharing any information.” There’s a rumbling in the distance and the first drops of rain splat on his three-piece suit. “Would you like to go below to get out of the rain? I have a few questions. Maybe you can help me.” I climb down the companionway. He grabs the handrail with a hard grip as he steps below. He takes the chair at my computer. I slide the hatch cover back in place and sit opposite him. A heavy gust of wind hits the boat causing him to swing around in the chair, losing his grip on the computer table. He begins pulling at his collar and his eyes dart around the cabin.

“Emily told me she was having trouble getting her account information off the computer,” I say.

“I’m not at liberty to discuss another person’s accounts.”

“How long ago did she change the beneficiary? Can you tell me that?”

“Did she share the whole problem with you or are you just a nosey sort?” He frowns. “I found her to be tedious and careless. That's why she couldn't keep up with her reports!" Lightning crashes overhead. His shallow breathing stops for a moment.

Emily was never careless about anything. I suspect the problem is with his reports. That's when I realize he came to find out how much I know. As his eyes recognize my understanding of a motive, he pulls a small pistol from his jacket pocket. That's when I stop breathing.

This gets us back to him, holding a gun on me. Even though the rain has cooled the air, I start to sweat through my t-shirt. Silent alarms ring in my ears. He's queasy and I need to take advantage of that.

"Your message indicated you knew more — and now I see, you do. Two snoopy, smart teachers are a bad combination. I need to buy a little more time." His eyes roll backward as the boat bangs against the dock.

"You've embezzled from more teachers than just Emily, haven't you?" He doesn't notice me looking for something, besides words, to use in my defense.

"A few years ago, I started getting checks from the board of education, by mistake. My weakness was in cashing that first check. Have you any idea how many teachers sign up for payroll deduction with my company?" Perspiration pops on his high forehead and top lip. His pale face makes the red hair above his ears look like misplaced earmuffs.

He continues his explanation. "It was so simple. I sent out the quarterly reports. No one complains if they think they're making money." He reaches for a handkerchief. "I'm not going to jail." He dabs his face, "I wouldn't last." The boat takes another roll toward the dock.

My ears ring, but I continue the questions, hoping to postpone the inevitable. "No one ever noticed false reports?"

"No. Before, I could always explain. She wasn't satisfied in talking with me about the problem. She sent messages to the home office." Briefly, his anger overcomes his nausea. "Now I have to leave town." He smiles thinking of something amusing. "You never took advantage of tax-deferred savings, Mrs. Connelly, but you won't need it now."

Blood begins to pound in my head as my face flushes with anger. When I'm nervous, I pop senseless jokes. He can't kill me; I'm almost at retirement age! "People live here, beside me. They'll call the police when they hear that gun."

He tut-tuts me, wiggling his gun hand, "Silencer." The man's like Captain Kangaroo, pulling a potato from another pocket! "I saw this on CSI and it works."

That gets me to thinking. What have I got to lose? He's too busy turning green to notice my range of sight. Two-Ton rubs against his ankle, startling Demsey into looking down.

I reach across, grabbing Mama's iron skillet as he tries to focus back in my direction. He never knows what struck him.

Speed dialing 911, I find some duct tape. By the time sirens blare into the parking lot, he's trussed tighter than a jury-rigged tiller. Duly impressed, Detective Thomas Wyles watches an unfortunate police officer assist the groggy, now puking-in-my-cockpit Dick Demsey, off my boat. I'll clean up his mess, content in thinking about all that red hair being yanked out when they pull off the tape.

Tom, as I call him now, drops by occasionally. Sometimes he buys me a burger. Sometimes we take a sail up the river. I bought Two-Ton some new catnip mousies. School's out and I'm stocking Aldeberan for my trip south.

A DAY WITH PETER JENNINGS

Catching a breath, I lean on the walking stick. A shadow crosses my sandaled dust-covered toes and a bottle of water appears. "You look like you could use this," says a familiar voice. I lean back, eyes traveling from his comfortable-looking shoes up long trousered legs into a familiar face.

I drink eagerly, watching him twist his plastic lid, gulp down the entire bottle, replace the lid and look behind my perch to a stone wall.

"Thank you." I pour a bit of water on a kerchief and dab my face.

The seasoned correspondent looks back and nods. "Your first time in Jerusalem." He states it more than asks.

"The children are grown and my grandkids don't need me. I promised after recovering from the stroke, I'd travel." He turns to walk away. Following, like a child pursuing Santa, I stuff the remaining water and guide book into my backpack. He slows when he notices my limp.

No teams of camera men or bodyguards are visible. He's just out for a walk. "Would you mind if I tag along?" He doesn't object.

The man stops to watch children running by and admires their exuberance. "Children are the same all over the world."

"My grandchildren play the same games," I dodge the last child. "I miss them."

He shoves my cheerless thoughts away by asking, "Where else have you traveled lately? You talk like someone who's been away from home a while." He's always the information gatherer.

"Oh, Peter. I can call you Peter, can't I?" He beams a nice smile. "I left home three months ago and I've been to Scotland, England, France, and Italy. Is it possible to be traveled out?"

"I never tire of travel, but I miss my family," he says. Walking, we compare our observations of familiar kirks, cathedrals, chapels, and shrines. He talks about those he's seen in the Orient and Africa. Peter's religious observations would seduce a classroom theologian.

The rest of the day, we visit temples and shrines, pastures, and riversides. We walk among olive and fig trees and take a bus to Bethlehem, where we eat lunch. The girls back home will be envious when they find out Peter Jennings bought lunch!

The afternoon fades and we find ourselves back in Jerusalem. Selfishly, I don't want the day to end. Peter leans against a doorway. Is he tired? "Would you like to walk the path Jesus took to Golgotha?" He knows the way.

At that moment, I have a call of nature. The urgency is embarrassing. I stop and he looks back. "I have to go," I explain.

"So do I." He lifts his hand in a salute.

I blink. A male nurse is adjusting my catheter. The late afternoon sun glares into the hospital room. I try shielding my eyes, but one arm doesn't obey. "What day is it?" I ask.

He nods, picks up the clipboard noting the time. "I should be asking you that question. Don't you remember?" The nurse waits patiently as I glance around. The daily paper I'd read earlier, is folded on the bed. Peter's face is on the front page.

"It's Thursday," I tell him. "When can I go home? I've got a trip to plan." Smoothing the bed sheet with the good hand, I struggle to sit up.

A perky physical therapist enters the room. "You can go home as soon as I get you walking better. Feel like a stroll down the hall?" She brings shoes over to the bedside and lowers the railing.

It's not every day one gets to tour the Holy Land with Peter Jennings. I listened as he compiled Biblical history, editing it -- as he did every evening on television. I've thought a lot about that day with Peter. For me, the hospital dream was a trip preview. For Peter, I think he was cramming for a final exam.

PREACHER'S DAUGHTER

Sweating and heart pounding, I spit out the last verse, "And Jacob begat Joseph the husband of Mary, of whom was born Jesus, who is called Christ." My Sunday School chair digs a ridge in the back of my legs. James Barry sticks out his tongue at me and Ernie Spratt hiccups. Mrs. Meadows wipes her nose in the flowered hankie she grasps in her hand when it's not stuck under her Bulova watchband. I sit down. The extra crinoline Mama made me wear causes the front of my dress to puff up. I hate it and these damn lacey socks. I can't wait to be in junior high when I can wear stockings, plaid skirts and matching sweaters like my older sister.

"Very good, Carrie Leigh," Mrs. Meadows doesn't smile because her twisted tooth shows. Mama says she's self-conscious about it. "Does anyone else want to try their recitation today?" A quiet hangs in the room usually droning with under-breath words and chair fidgeting. Mrs. Meadows tries to sound enthusiastic. "Well.

If no one's ready, let's begin our Sword Drill." We hold our Bibles like a sword hilt as she calls out a Bible book, chapter and verse. Everyone participates in teams. It's the only time I *ever* get picked first.

I'm the preacher's daughter, Carrie Leigh McDuffy. I can't run, throw, catch, or dodge a ball. I break fingernails, jamb thumbs, and skin my knees whenever a ball's involved. I don't like getting dirty so don't ask me to play your stupid damn ball games. I like the word "damn." I don't say it in front of Mama or, heaven forbid, Daddy, but inside my head, "damn" bubbles around just fine. Next year I may start saying "shit" -- under my breath.

I wake up early every morning, pull my Bible off my desk, and memorize passages. Mrs. Meadows says, "If the Russians take over the world, all the Bibles will be burned in the center of town. We have to learn Bible passages so we can have them 'in our hearts' for when that time comes." Daddy thinks that's nonsense, but he encourages me to memorize anyway, including the order of the books of the Bible, which is the reason I'm first choice by Sword Drill team captains. John Mark Lewis -- he's the class president - calls my name. I beam over to his side and hold my gold-engraved, soft, white leather King James Bible like it's Excalibur. John Mark can be my King Arthur anytime.

Belinda May Faulks pouts when she hears James Barry call out her name. She has the hots for John Mark. I caught them kissing under the choir loft stairwell two Sundays ago. "Vulgar woman," Mama says. "If a girl kisses in public, no telling what she's up to in private." But in the sixth grade, I've never been kissed, much less got to tongue touch. I know about that. I hear my big sister, Sarah Vargas, whispering on the hall phone.

More names get called and the whole class moves chairs around until the front lines of opposing teams are kneed and toed together waiting for the call to arms. All this team selecting and room re-arranging succeeds in using up ten more minutes of class time.

Belinda May steps over, squashing down on my toes with her prissy-bowed flats. Her lips pinch into a prim line, like a squashed caterpillar, as she tries to make me holler. I ignore her even though she's messing up my new shoes. I make sure she sees me lean into John Mark's shoulder. She immediately stops.

"John Mark," I sigh, fluttering my pale eyelashes. "I'm glad you chose me first." I smirk at Belinda May. She glares back. He's peeking inside his Bible where he inserts his finger in the table of contents. That's cheating. He cheats all the time. He talked Betty Thompson into doing his schoolwork and the teachers look the other way. His daddy's the school board chairman.

"We're gonna win this," I say. At last he looks into my eyes. I hope he notices they match my green dress.

"Sure," he wipes his nose with a finger that isn't stuffed in his Bible and glances over to Belinda May.

Mrs. Meadows moves the podium to the center of the room. "Are y'all ready?" She opens her Bible to a verse and says, "Matthew 4:14."

I crack my white leather and flip over to the New Testament. Belinda May has a Bible with little named stepping stairs notched into its side. She licks her thumb, turning a page. At the same time she shoots an arm up. "I have it, Miz Meadows."

Pleased as punch, she reads the verse out loud, ignoring my dropped mouth and raised eye brows.

Disaster! My King James is glued together. If I turn the pages too quickly, I rip the gold-edged tissue pages. It looks like someone put boogers, God forbid, all through my Bible.

Oh, please let it be tiny pieces of gum. This is my Confirmation Bible. Daddy presented it to me when I turned ten. John Mark eyes me like I'm Quasimodo. I shrug and peel my pages apart as the rest of the class continues their battle.

My team loses. "Shit!" It pops out of my mouth. Someone giggles. Mrs. Meadows pretends she didn't hear it. I can feel the heat rise in my cheeks, freckles surfacing around my eyes like a raccoon's mask. The church bell chimes, calling everyone to the sanctuary, including Mrs. Meadows, who now has her flowered hankie over her mouth.

I stand as Ernie Spratt sneaks back into the classroom. He's in the eighth grade. He takes my gummy white leather gold-engraved King James, leans down, and kisses me. His lips are cool and dry. I never

noticed his long lashes or gold-flecked eyes
before. He turns and walks away like
nothing happened, taking my King James.
My heart pounds and my Sunday School
chair digs a ridge in the back of my legs.

WHILE YOU WERE OUT

"Sister, I don't know how you can spend so much time out in the garden and then linger, arranging your flowers like you do." Margaret Anne pulls a fresh cobbler apron down over her head and smoothes the boxy shoulders over her print housedress. "While you were out fiddling with your tulips and daffodils, I boned three whole chickens and chopped them into little pieces, the way Mama likes, for making her chicken salad sandwiches. This is going to be our best Spring Tea yet, don't you think?"

Both retired teachers live with their mother in the century-old home. Mary Jo, smiling at her younger sister, makes three trips from the back porch carrying cut-glass vases filled with fresh flowers. The fragrances of narcissus and honeysuckle linger.

"Now, Margaret Anne," Mary Jo concedes, "Mama always said no one can cut up chicken better than you." She arranges the containers on mantels and the sideboard, and sets two arrangements aside for the tables. "I forgot to pick up our cut-lace tablecloths. I'll drive over to Belington's Laundry and pick them up. They do such a good job of pressing Mama's linens." She grabs the keys to the Ford and sashays out the front door. With the exception of gray eyes, her trim body has little in common with her sister's soft padded one. Margaret Anne continues her morning chores.

"What took you so long, Sister? While you were out, I waxed the dining room table, dusted the mantels over both fireplaces, vacuumed the parlor, and helped Mama polish the salad forks. We stacked all the clear salad plates on the sideboard so you can finish laying out the tables. The silver punch bowl is shined and the lime sherbet punch just needs to be mixed." Smugly, Margaret Anne re-pins a bobby pin screwed curl back under her nylon bonnet. "I washed the punch cups, so you may as well bring out that tray from the kitchen." She fans her dumpling face with a plump hand as she watches her sister straighten the tablecloths and dress the tables.

"Margaret Anne, I'm running to the beauty parlor. Jessie said she'd help me put my hair up in that new French twist, if I came before lunch. Don't do everything. I'll help when I get back." Watching herself in the hall mirror Mary Jo ties a bright scarf around her neck.

"I declare Mary Jo, while you were out I filled the platters with Mama's seven-day pickles, stuffed celery, and eggs. I'm glad you helped me with those deviled eggs yesterday. I put little sprigs of parsley along the side. I wanted you to look them over. You are so good at arranging things," Margaret Anne points with her chin as she creams her hands. "Take those to the table.

Don't forget the silver-footed bowls of nuts and the tiny tray of cheese straws. I'm going upstairs to change clothes and fix my hair." Taking off her apron, she folds it over a kitchen chair. She huffs up to the stair landing and stares, wondering what else she's supposed to do before three o'clock. Shaking her frowning face at the dust-free window sill, she continues her assent.

Shortly thereafter, Margaret Anne descends wearing her white open-toed sensible laced shoes and a floral polyester shirtwaist dress she made herself. With powdered face, rouged cheeks and a sprinkling of Lily of the Valley dusting powder, she steps out onto the front porch. Within the hour, she admonishes her older sister one last time. "Sister while you were out in the breakfast room folding napkins, I swept off the porch, rearranged the hanging geranium baskets, and carried folding chairs into the parlor." Margaret Anne pushes a gray curl behind her pink pearl-sheathed ear. She dabs her chin and forehead with her hankie and tucks it back into her belt.

Even though its spring, the smells of past hickory fires remain in the dimly lit parlor. A thick red Oriental carpet pads her step as she crosses to the wooden-floored hall to check the tables one last time. She pops a butter cream mint in her mouth. Last week, she cut them on Mama's marble slab after they cooled. Mary Jo fans the napkins next to the forks and smoothes the tablecloth again.

The door bell rings announcing the first of their guests. Mama sits in the front porch swing. Margaret Anne watches while her sister promenades through the gaggle of ladies. They preen in their store bought silks, crepes, and chiffons -- short jacketed suits, draped floral sheaths, pastel dusters crowned with prissy feathered or gay flowered hats. Creaks of the old house are muffled as the soft laughter, gossip, and often-told stories float through the downstairs rooms.

Margaret Anne finds herself in the kitchen making sure empty platters are refilled and empty plates and cups are washed without breaking. Easing her tired back against a kitchen chair, after everyone leaves she sighs. "Well, Sister, we sure did Mama proud. Everything looked so nice, don't you think? While you were out mingling, like you do so well, Mrs. Adrienne Harris dropped back here.

She complimented us on the lovely tea. She says it was the best we ever had!" Margaret Anne beams. Cooling herself, she lifts the damp bodice away from her ample bosom. "I told her, 'Mrs. Harris, you're so kind to come back here just to say that. We love showing off Mama's house. Thank you. It was nothing. Really.'"

THE COURIERS

Sheriff Conner leads Lillian Beneridge into the interrogation room. He feels rather than sees his deputy and the district attorney behind a mirrored wall. The smell of bleach and body odor draws Woodruff's bushy eyebrows into a frown as he drops a notepad, pencil, and tape recorder on to the worn table. Pulling out a metal chair, he offers her a seat. "Now, Mrs. Beneridge, would you like coffee or a soda?"

"Coffee, please." She fiddles with the gnawed corner of the table. "I rarely brew coffee on our boat. I can't remember when I made a cup." One side of her mouth sags as she speaks. After a minute or two, a female officer slips into the room bringing Lillian a mug of coffee.

With skinny arms folded behind her back, the deputy leans against the wall. She has dark eyes, smooth black skin, and an Afro-buzz.

Lillian studies the deputy's creased uniform and patent leather gun-belt. The deputy reminds her of a cricket. She tastes the coffee and makes a face. "My, that's a bit strong, but thank you, dear." She takes a long sip before placing the mug down. Pressing both hands on the tabletop, she tries to rub the surface smooth.

The sheriff punches the tape recorder button, "Interview with Lillian Beneridge concerning confiscated boat on Legaway Creek, August 12th. Sheriff Conner Woodruff and Deputy Varner present. Please tell us about your boat trip, Ma'am."

She tries to clear her gravelly throat. "Our boat's name is *Miss Lily*. We leave every year -- at the end of hurricane season. Dave and I began our trip like we always do, except this last time we woke up to a heavy fog. We started the engine, weighed anchor, and slid into the early morning mist."

Like a proud child she explains, "When it's foggy, I sit on the bow and let my legs dangle over the bowsprit. It's my job to guide Dave between day marks, crab pots, and boats.

"We've cruised for over thirty years. People ask us why we do it. Why not? It's something we both enjoy. Do you have a boat, Sheriff?"

He leans forward to adjust the microphone. "Yes, ma'am, I do."

She nods, confirming he's a boat person. "We never regretted our choice to live aboard. A bond develops between two people when you live aboard. It's hard to describe. We know what the other's thinking." She blushes, "It's a passionate connection. You can't appreciate it unless you've cruised." The sheriff dips his head as if he understands. Her clouded eyes search for Dave. She licks her lips. Sunspots on her skin hint of the years spent aboard. Her hair tied up off her neck struggles to maintain a bun. A knotted bandana hangs from her neck.

"Dave and I have been spliced together for 52 years. Is this what you want to know?" He nods as she continues. "We used to have a forty-foot sailboat, but we sold that for a small trawler. Our cruising range shortened when we turned 65, not because we lost our ability to navigate, but our retirement pool dwindled during that market drop.

"Well, Dave saw a classified ad in a cruising magazine about seniors making money while living aboard. You wouldn't believe all the inspections and forms we went through." She winks, this time breaking into a lop-sided smile. "Dave knows all the details; I'm just the bookkeeper and navigator. *He's* the captain.

"Part of the agreement is that we haul out the boat in Georgia. Well, my goodness, we do that anyway to have the bottom painted. When we get up to the Chesapeake, they pull her out again. Just between you and me, I don't mind. It's nice to spend a few days ashore. They put us up in a nice place. The man pays us good money so we can afford to use dockhands to do all our work, even oil changes and topside scrubbing."

"Ma'am, can I ask what you make off these runs?" The sheriff wants names and numbers.

She resumes her own line of thought. "This income takes a load off my mind. I can't remember what we make without my notebook. Dave knows. I get more forgetful each day." While she talks, she aligns the tape recorder, pad, and pencil in a row. Frowning, she re-arranges them perpendicular to the table edge. "Dave prods me to do mind games. He asks me to name marinas, our favorite restaurants, places we visit, and grocery stores. I sometimes forget where the refrigerator is or where we stow clothes, but he makes stickers to help me.

"Last year, I think it was, we paid cash for the North Carolina townhouse." Her mind goes elsewhere; her unfocused eyes look beyond the sheriff. "Our boat's name is *Miss Lily*. We leave every year -- at the end of hurricane season. I'm good at seeing crab pots. 'Dave, there's a crab pot at two o'clock.'" Her arm sweeps toward the mirrored wall. "He'd ease the boat around the confounded thing and we'd glide back to the side of the channel.

"Getting old has set-backs, like loss of agility, this forgetfulness, achy joints, and pills." The Sheriff shifts in his chair as Deputy Varner sits beside him. "Water hyacinths drift in the Waccamaw River and Dismal Swamp. It's lovely, have you ever been there?"

"No ma'am. Can you tell us about your employers?" Deputy Varner prods Lillian.

She ignores the question as her mind replays the trip. "In the fall, heading south, we keep up with the Indian summer. Traveling down river, murky waters turn brackish. Closer to the ocean, the salt brindles the air. Did you know traveling by boat slows time?" She inhales trying to find sea air in the stuffy room. Lillian pulls a strand of hair behind her ear, then focuses on the woman deputy.

"Do you have a head? That coffee went right through me." Officer Varner escorts her to the bathroom. A few minutes later Lillian continues, "Now, that feels better. I don't suppose you have some crackers? When my blood sugar gets low, my head gets even fuzzier." She feels movement behind the mirror and someone else appears with a package of Cheese Nabs.

"Why, thank you." Her fingers fumble with the wrapped crackers. She takes a bite, trailing crumbs from the corner of her mouth down her blouse.

"Mrs. Beneridge, you were telling us about the people you meet in Baltimore, where we found you." Sheriff Woodruff leans forward, trying to capture her wandering eyes with his own.

"Oh, I don't know their names, son. They gave us a cell phone and call telling us where to bring the boat. Now that we have a shallow draft boat without a 50-foot mast overhead we can squeeze up any shallow river." She stops and her eyes stare like a blank television between commercials.

A moment later, her eyes refocus on the crackers clutched in her hands. "My mind drifts sometimes, forgive me. The doctor told us to consider living ashore full time. This is our last cruise." She timidly covers her mouth, "Before my stroke, my smile took up my whole face. My droopy mouth embarrasses me.

"I have accidents when I'm cooking. My husband prefers us to buy meals where we can. We stop where there's baked goods and bread for sandwiches. We pay cash for all our fuel and meals. Imagine the clerk's surprise when I hand over a crisp hundred-dollar bill!" Like a child whispering a secret, "They always pay us in cash. One time Dave figured there must be over a hundred couriers on the waterway."

Again her mind drifts. "Going north in the spring, the jasmine and gardenia fragrance is overpowering. I just love it."

She frowns, "They boarded our boat at a narrow place between the Albemarle

Sound and Norfolk. Both the Marine Patrol and Coast Guard's boats blocked the river, stopping the larger cruisers and boarding smaller boats. They glide up to our side on an Avon, you know, the orange inflatable. A couple of men hop aboard. I can't tell whether they're looking for drugs or terrorists. We've seen dogs sniffing. Dave always has our registration and last inspection papers ready.

"One time a young man told me, 'Your lavender reminds me of my grandmother.' Well I never! You know how the bilge and holding tank have an odor?" She waits for him to respond. He nods, tapping the notepad with a thick finger. "Well, I use lavender to hide the smell. I use cayenne pepper where I don't want varmints. Their dogs don't like it, but it stops the bugs!"

She narrows her eyes. "It was awful. All those people and sirens. Old fiberglass burns fast, any sailor will tell you. Dave told me to jump in the dinghy while he went below for something. My ears still hurt." Her slender hands try to press out the explosion.

"Today was different. Why do you suppose that was?" Lillian leans back in her chair and re-crosses her leg.

"That's why you're here Mrs. Beneridge. We need to know what happened today." The sheriff loses patience.

Batting invisible gnats, Lillian struggles to continue, "We've got a cellular phone aboard. They call us and tell Dave where to go. Sometimes the folks are impatient, but we didn't sign up to be on a time clock. 'No sir, they'll just have to wait on their deliveries,' Dave was adamant."

The woman stops and looks at the uniformed officers. She clears her throat. "Are you sure Dave's dead?"

"Yes ma'am. Is there someone we need to call for you? Do you know anyone in the area -- maybe these people who call you?" He tries again to siphon new information from her clouded mind.

Her brow furrows as she concentrates. A delicate bead of perspiration forms on her top lip. "I don't think I can drive the boat without Dave. Our boat's the *Miss Lily* and we leave each year, just after the hurricane season."

The sheriff leaves her with his deputy and steps outside the detaining room. The air-conditioner circulates the smells of burnt coffee, copy machines, and people.

A tall district attorney steps out of the adjoining room. The man removes a handkerchief from his hip pocket and wipes sweat from his forehead and neck. "He must have figured we were onto him. It was booby-trapped or he rigged it himself. Damn, what a scam! Do you think she's right? Are there hundreds of cruisers, delivering drugs on our waterways so they can earn their spending money?"

The sheriff smirks, "I've no idea. Her husband's dead and the hull burned to the waterline. There's no clue as to how much stuff they were carrying, where they were going or who's running the operation. He shifts his holster above his thick waist. "Tell me what you want me to do with her."

"Book her. We'll get our psychiatrist over to evaluate her." The DA strolls down the hall; a fluorescent light buzzes overhead.

Later that evening, Sheriff Woodruff's chair creaks as he signs the papers on his desk. He opens desk drawers and sorts out his personal items, piling them into a box. From his window, he watches bruised skies reflect purple and red on the Chesapeake Bay. Lifting the telephone receiver, he dials home. "Marjorie, how you doing, Sugar?" He leans back in his chair, propping his feet on the desk, and listens to the highlights of her day. "I'll be home soon. You know how we've talked about moving aboard when I retire? Well, I've been thinking on it. I'll tell you more when I get home. Bye, now. I love you, too." He tosses a spiraled notebook into his box. Its cover reads, "Courier's Log of the Motor Vessel, *Miss Lily*." Heaving the box on his shoulder, he wets his lips to whistle a tune, "*What do you do with a drunken sailor early in the morning?*"

MAN IN THE MIRROR

I sucked the last taste of bourbon from the ice in my glass and signaled the bartender to bring me another. My mind was as empty as my glass. It was May 1937. I was a young *Herald Times* reporter, on assignment in Frankfort the past three months because I spoke German. Sitting in the bar most of the afternoon, I noticed people crowding into the lobby, dining room, and bar like errant metal filings drawn to a magnet.

Roosevelt was championing anyone fighting the evils of Fascism and Communism. Britain's Prince Edward was about to be crowned. Jews no longer practiced medicine, dentistry or any other profession. They were being corralled into camps, but we ignored it. Joe Lewis was fighting his way to a Heavyweight Championship and I — wanted to go home.

A young couple and three children sat near the door. An elderly couple whispered back and forth - while he read, she knitted. Glasses, china, and silverware clinked at the tables. Wealthy millionaire-types, glamorous babes and a tanned cowboy entered the bar. He saddled up on the stool next to me and in German, ordered a drink. I counted about 50 people and knew something besides the foreign-cigarette smoke hazed around the bar.

Another couple entered the dining room. Not looking left or right they found their way to a back table, beneath a lacquered-framed mirror. From my perch on the bar stool, I peered around a column to watch their conversation. He interrogated her and she fed him information like a tantalizing lover.

His cuff links and her gold earrings winked at each other as the sun moved across the window. They carefully screened their conversation. His hat slanted down when he talked and she turned her head, but I could see her and the velveteen cloche on her dark hair in the mirror. Her sultry brunette head tipped and nodded. Her tailored suit fit like leaves concealing a blossom.

He used the mirror to watch the people in the dining room and when she wasn't looking, he memorized her face, engraving every curve and texture in his own mind. She pretended not to notice.

Catching my own reflection in their mirror, I watched my head dodge back and forth behind the column. I tried, unsuccessfully, to read their lips. All my instincts told me *they* were *my* next headline.

I heard my name and without changing my gaze, raised my hand to call the page. Her eyes glanced at mine in the mirror. She placed her hand on his to stub out his cigarette and reached for her bag. He threw money on the table as they walked away.

I asked the young page about the crowd. His excited voice shared the information, "They've purchased tickets on the Zeppelin and are leaving for the bus." As I tipped him, I noted the draining room.

Hailing a cab, I followed the bus as far as the hangar, but guards blocked my entry. After returning to the hotel, I opened my letter. Enclosed within my packet were train tickets and ship passage. I was going home.

Four days later, bold headlines of the daily paper read, "**Hindenburg Crashes – 37**

Die." I memorized the statistics. The Hindenburg was as long as the Titanic. She cruised at 78 mph. This was her first trans-Atlantic crossing. The entire tragedy took 34 seconds. Thirty-nine of the 61 crew members lived. Ninety-seven people and two dogs were on board. When my ship docked in New York City, I tracked down the surviving 23 passengers. I've monitored them ever since. What made the passengers do the unthinkable? They walked through fire while their bodies burned, jumped from fiery hell to the ground 15-40 feet away, and survived.

Nelson Morris, a meatpacking executive from Chicago told me, "I thought I heard a crack, like a service rifle." He held up his bandaged hands, "I pushed through white-hot beams of steel to get past the flames." His actress wife sat at his side, offering water through a straw. She hadn't traveled with him that time.

William Leuchtenberg's eyes burned shut in the explosion. When led from the wreckage, he tried to return for his false teeth.

Philip Mangone, a well-know dress designer, traveled to Europe on business and for treatment for a stomach ailment. He avoided misfortune in 1915, when he cancelled his ticket on the *Lusitania*. Mangone spent the entire trip on the Hindenberg, in his cabin, nursing a cold and fever. After recovering from burns, he continued as an America designer until his death in 1957.

Comedian/acrobat, Joseph Spah a.k.a "Ben Dova," dangled by one hand from the balloon's window edge, letting go when the dirigible dropped within 40 feet of the ground. He held up a plaster encased foot and pointed with a cane, "Now I really have an act to follow!" The experienced acrobat enamored passengers on the flight. I wondered why Gestapo officers shadowed him on his entire European tour.

Young 28-year old Herbert James O'Laughlin, after emerging burn-free from the wreckage, ran soot-covered to the hangar. He wired his mother, "Arrived safely." The operator didn't charge him for the telegram.

Mrs. Matilde Doehner pushed her three children out of the burning maze where they toppled onto the ground, before she jumped. "The stewardess took Werner's truck away from him on the first day. It was a toy with Mickey Mouse driving it! She said it could cause a spark." Mrs. Doehner sued for the loss of her husband and daughter. In the melted remains, investigators found the remains of the toy truck. The stewardess, Emilie Imhof, perished in the fire.

Margaret Mather, my cloche-wearing sultry woman, spent her summers on Cape Cod; her father was a wealthy New York attorney. "I sat in my seat watching beautiful tongues of fire leap from all sides. I held my coat up around my face. I could feel the flames on my back and in my hair." She pulled the bedclothes up to her cheeks while burn medicine oozed down her hands. "I couldn't find my purse. Someone asked if I was ready to leave. We jumped together. I don't remember his face." She moved to Italy, but returned to New York every spring to buy a new wardrobe.

Writer, Leonard Adelt, commented, "It sounded like someone had opened a beer bottle, not loud. Then we were surrounded by flames." Adelt and his wife, Gertrude Stolte, were friends with well-known Jewish writers. The couple managed to evade the "re-education of journalists at Dachau." He was working on a book, about the great Zeppelins, that published later that year. They returned to Germany where he died in an Allied raid over Dresden with 70,000 other citizens.

Otto and Elsa Ernst were planning to stay a week in New York City. Mrs. Ernst described that afternoon, "It was a beautiful day. We circled New York City several times. We took pictures of the Statue of Liberty and the Empire State Building. The Dodgers were playing the Pittsburgh Pirates at Ebbets Field! We finally arrived at Lakehurst, N. J. and we were standing, reaching for our bags, preparing to leave. When the fire started, Otto held my hand. Like one of your Hollywood movies, when the stern touched the earth, the gangplank dropped. We walked down the walkway arm in arm without a scratch. Otto kept hitting the flames that lit our clothes." Burning debris fell around them as they walked.

In 1937, jitterbug marathons were the rage, Spencer Tracey won the Academy Award for *Captains Courageous*, Hormel invented SPAM and — Amelia Earhart vanished. The year 1937 still pre-occupies me even though it's been over 65 years. If I walk into a smoke-filled room, I still see myself in the lacquered-framed mirror and the haunting faces of the Zeppelin's passengers.

(This is fact and fiction or *faction*. I used various web-sites and resources, including the Hindenburg's web site for information. Any errors are mine and I apologize.)

HAUNTING KISS

He digs on his knees, in the dirt around the grave marker, tugging at weeds and picking up bits of trash. A tattoo peeks from one sleeve. He drives his truck here, parking it under the water oaks near the family plot. Age, cigarettes, sun, and guilt wrinkle his face, like a tan raisin.

Last week, ropey arms poured concrete to anchor a flagpole. Today, a flag blows overhead as trays of chrysanthemums await interment. "Asa Mann Guthrie and Muriel Mason Guthrie, beloved parents now rest with Jesus." Did he miss their final days — or years?

Mornings and evenings, I walk the graveyard among fresh, silk, and plastic flowers. New markers appear. Lambs, angels, obelisks, rectangles remind the living -- of the dying. Can he hear his mother's voice above the rattling lawn mower? When the geese fly overhead, does he recall his father's cough?

He no longer looks like someone guys hung out with and girls ogled like they did in high school. Does he remember the smell of purple printed tests, chalk dust, biology labs, and the school lunchroom? Does Mr. Big still tease the ladies? He once acted cool. Now, he looks coolly from hardened eyes.

The breeze shifts to northeast bringing the marsh musk. Does he smell burning leaves and does it remind him of Vietnam's burned flesh? He once danced to Beach Music, swiveling his hips and shuffling his shoes along the sandy floor. This evening, his radio casts honky-tonk music into the cemetery.

I've not given him a second glance in 40 years. One hot day, near the end of the school year, he walked toward me. He wore a madras shirt, white duck pants, and English Leather. I wore a pink seersucker dress. Never saying a word, he lowered his head and kissed me. Was it a dare or impulse? His whim burns in my memory.

Deep-sunk eyes glance away as I pass. He lights a cigarette and picks a bit of tobacco from his tongue. Would he recognize me among all the ones he kissed before and after? Would he shiver if I appear, touching my lips to his? No, I haven't a ghost of a chance.

PATRICIA ANNE'S SONG

"Me name's Dan O'Keefe, Mrs., I'm a fixer of t'ings and a marvelous story weaver. I mean ya' no harm and I'll not be after a handout. I'll work for me keep." The burly man stood inside the door, oilskins dripping on her floor while the storm raged outside. Her dog, Peg, sniffed at the man then slumped down by the electric heater. "I need a dry place to sleep out of dis terrible storm."

"I wouldn't put me dog out on a night like this. I'll do no less for a man. Come get dry. You can sleep here." She indicated an old couch along the wall. He began peeling off the yellow slicker and suspendered pants. His dark oiled sweater was worn ragged at the collar and elbows. "You can dry off in our loo. You'll find towels under the sink and don't go making a mess." Ringlets of graying wet hair curled over his collar and through his coarse beard. Thick sausage-like fingers brushed drops of rain from his flannel shirt.

She'd watched his purposeful descent to her house for the past hour when he crested the hill a few kilometers away. He made his way directly to her door across fields of heather and stone fences striding through the flickering bursts of lightning and rain. While she kept an eye on his approach, she fed her shuttle back and forth across the loom, banging the beater to tighten and straighten the threads after each pass. Her toes tapped the treadles lifting the design-making heddles across the warp in a continuous tempo. Before her husband died, she used the loom's rhythm to accompany her singing. Both her husband and her father had loved her singing.

"Mum, who's that man? What does he want?" Her son called from his bedroom door.

"No need to worry about the man. Our Peg's a good judge of people. See how's she's wagging her tail now? Have you finished your schoolwork? If so, call your sister to supper and both of you set the table."

She loved the way she could see the kitchen and living area of the house from her weaving space. Her husband had added this section of the house, building shelves for her yarns and a well-lit place for her loom and computer. Mrs. McFarland was startled to see the huge man had quietly returned and was gazing at her woolen skeins.

"They're beautiful, Mrs., the colors. I can see the sky and the sea in your work." The vibrant yarns were organized -- deep blues to pale mists and crimson sunsets to cream. "Did you know you weave the sea, Mrs.?" His eyes were gentle as he gazed at the cloth on her loom. He stood so close she could smell the storm on his clothes. "'Tis an angry sea you're weaving today." His finger touched the thick blue, black and green yarns. "That strand of knobby white running there is like spindrift on a rolling sea."

"Mr. O'Keefe you're a story weaver for sure and wouldn't you know I have a generator that needs your fixing tomorrow but for now let's eat. Join us for supper, there's plenty if you like vegetable stew?" She rose from her loom and stretched back, bracing her hands on her waist. Her short wavy hair and sweater shrouded her slender neck.

"*Arrgh*, a vegetable stew. You're a woman after me own heart, Mrs. McFarland." He followed her into the kitchen area. There he met a wisp of a girl with fiery eyes. Jaw pushed out and eyes closed to a slit, she stood with her hands clutching a floppy toy. Her dark red hair sprayed ringlets over her shoulders.

"Who's this little person defending her kitchen so bravely against a stranger who means her no harm." He squatted down in front of the child to ask her name.

"My name's Patricia Anne Mary Margaret Colleen Elizabeth McFarland. Who are you?" the seven-year-old demanded.

Defensively he held up his hands, "Saints preserve us! Me name's Daniel Joseph O'Keefe. At your service, m'lady." He bowed deeply, "But you tell me why does such a small girl have such a big name?"

"Because I'm the last. I have me Mum's name and me Mum's mum's name and me Da's mum's name."

"And where did you get all that beautiful red hair?"

Her hand fingered a strand of curls. "I get it from me Mum, but she cut hers off when me Da passed." She spit out the words as if she'd said them before. Her eyes dropped to his hand. She pointed to the stub that was his thumb and asked, "What happened to your finger?"

"Patricia Anne, mind your manners, young lady. The man is a guest in our home." Mrs. McFarland turned to the man, "You've met the charming daughter; this is my son, Sean and the dog's - Peg. Now put yourself down and join us here, Mr. O'Keefe."

"No harm done, Patricia Anne Mary Margaret Colleen Elizabeth. When we've e't I'll tell you the story of losing me finger and the day I quit being a fixer at sea and became a fixer on land."

After the meal, Dan O'Keefe inquired, "Mrs. McFarland, I don't suppose ya have a wee drop of something stronger in the house? The tea's fine but me old bones crave a different warmth." She went to the cabinet and searched for a bottle.

She poured a dollop of whiskey into his mug. "I'll not have a drunk in my house, Mr. O'Keefe, so I'll be minding the bottle." She walked back to her loom, bottle in hand.

He turned to the boy, "A fine name, Sean, a man's name. It has strength and courage in the sound of it." He rubbed a hand across his bearded face.

"It was me Da's name. I'd like to grow up and be a fisherman, but me Mum says no boats. She lost a father, a brother and a husband to the sea and doesn't want to lose a son. I'll go to engineering school in Cork. I'm good at mathematics."

"Are you now? I took you for a smart lad, but a boy without a boat is a sad thing. Fetch me duffle by the couch there." The boy dragged the canvas sack over to the table and watched the man dig into the lumpy bag.

He pulled a hand-carved sailing dory from his bag. "Here, now. This should do. I'm ready to be rid of it." He untied a cloth sack revealing a tiny mast, oars, bucket and crab pot.

"Why it's the grandest little boat I've ever seen. Thank you Mr. O'Keefe." The boy's hands ran over the carefully carved hull. Patricia Anne crawled up to look.

"Girlie, tell me now, what kind of animal is that you're huggin'? I've never seen the likes of it," O'Keefe eyed the rag toy.

"This is <u>my</u> horse. Mum made it from me Da's old shirt when she cut it down for Sean. See, he has ears, a mane, tail and a red heart. I sleep with him. It used to smell of me Da."

"But he has no eyes, child. How can he see?" She gave her horse and the man a perplexed look. "How 'bout if I make him some eyes? Would you like that?" Curls bouncing, she nodded her head. He pulled a piece of wood from the duffle then opened the knife blade. He sized off a space, notched the wood and began to carve.

Mrs. McFarland rose from her loom and eyed the man. "Would you want a bit more to drink, Mr. O'Keefe?" She smiled for the first time that evening, pouring him a finger of liquor. She returned to the rhythmic motions of her loom.

"Mrs. McFarland, thank you kindly. You're a weaving angel, y'are. Well, now I promised you two a story, didn't I? It begins five years ago. I always had a way with motors and fixing t'ings, like I said but I had a yearning for the sea. I'd hire out to boats as a fixer. I'd fix winches, diesel engines and I'd help with the fishing." His calloused hands worked the wood tenderly as if he was stroking a baby.

"I've worked boats out of Howth, Ardglass, and Baltimore. This last trip to sea, I'd come to County Donegal out from Killybegs with five others. It was mid-winter and the weather was colder than charity." As if on cue a mighty blast of wind and rain shuddered the house. "The sea was angry that year. She fought us tearing shrouds from stanchions one day and ripping nets open the next. The waves were like mountains and the cold so icy, the tears froze to your eyes." Mrs. McFarland slapped her beater gently, her feet lightly danced among her treadles.

"Many a night we'd sit by the stove and tell stories about our families. My first mate often talked about his family. He was a man with a deep love for his wife. He'd told me his wife's long red hair was so beautiful and strong it could pull a drowning man from the surf.

"One night, a storm hit us; so fierce the forward hatch cover ripped off. We struggled to cover that dark gaping mouth on our deck. It swallowed huge gulps of rain as we were thrown about like toys. The boat began to wallow in frightful gullies of water. Waves tossed us to the top of each crest then slammed us down.

"While we tried to cover that hatch, the rudder snapped. Without steering, we were lost. As the boat was beat apart, I was thrown overboard with the first mate. We had no life jacket between us. We wouldna' last thirty minutes if we hadn't grabbed hold to a piece of floating deck. We crawled as high as we could out of the water, but the surf pounded us with cold angry fists. We were going to die. My mate called to God to see after his wife and children.

He paused, "I don't remember much else. When I come 'round, a rescue boat was pulling me up. They found me floating on that missing hatch cover." O'Keefe finished carving the horse eyes and used his marlinspike to drill holes through them. "Want me to sew them on?" he asked the girl.

He interrupted his story to search in his duffle for a sewing kit. He threaded his needle and with the girl's help sewed the eyes in place. "There, now, Patricia Anne Mary Margaret Colleen Elizabeth, your horse can see." She studied the eyes, then hugged the horse closer as she waited for him to finish the story.

"I lost me thumb in that devilish storm. A bowline's a strong knot; you can throw one around a piling to pull in a boat or one around yourself for a life sling, but mind you don't catch your finger in the eye as it closes -- it'll chop off your thumb as sure as I'm sitting here. I must'a caught it in a line during that storm and didna' know it was gone. Well, now, I haven't set foot on a boat since. That small boat there, son, and the eyes I just carved, girlie, are me last pieces of that hatch board. So, that's the end of me tale."

Mrs. McFarland rose from her weaving bench and scooted her children off to bed. When she returned, she placed the bottle of whiskey on the table by the man. "Are your stories true, Mr. O'Keefe, or do you weave them as you go?"

"Well now, Mrs.," he poured himself a half cup more, "I'm a fixer of t'ings, remember. If you find truth in me stories, it's because you're looking for it." He drained his mug.

"Do you mind if I continue my work, Mr. O'Keefe? My weaving puts food on the table and I need to finish this shawl before I go to bed."

"No, Mrs., won't bother me none."

Outside the wind continued to batter the house.

After a few minutes, she paused, "Mr. O'Keefe?" He rolled over and sat up. "What was the name of that last fishing boat? Can you tell me that?" She waited, biting her bottom lip.

"She was *Patricia Anne's Song*, Mrs. McFarland; her name was *Patricia Anne's Song*.

A CATTY TALE

I usually avoid awkward positions as an accountant for Levine's Department Stores. I came into the stock room to get a couple of #2 pencils. As I broke open a package, pencils sprayed worse than a pick-up-stick drop. I scrambled to my knees as Mrs. Priscilla Levine walked in like a cat on the prowl. In my unlady-like position, I froze, hoping she'd pass without noticing me.

When Stanley Lassiter, the Vice President of Human Resources, came out of the bathroom, she pounced like a cat on a finch. She propped one leg up on a case of toilet paper, corralling him with her body, tapping his chest with long painted fingernails.

We all heard another flush behind the door. At that moment, I bumped my head on the stainless steel wire rack labeled "scissors, rulers, and assorted paper fasteners."

They stared at me, as I rose from the errant pencils search. She grabbed me, shoved me into Mr. Lassiter's arms, and stepped back as her hubby — Bud, finished drying his hands on his environmentally efficient wall-hanging blower.

Stanley Lassiter backed me into a rack of bathroom cleaning supplies. The smell of pine scented janitorial products will never be the same. It's hard to think about the man whose mouth is covering mine. We have an audience. He has wonderful lips and his hands move over my fanny like they've done it before. The Vice President of Lips, err, Human Resources has me in a very pleasant body clutch. As Mr. Resources is about to count my teeth with his tongue, he pulls back, blushes like a little boy, and says, "Oh, sorry, Bud. I can't seem to get enough of this lady. See you later, Liz." He winks at me and walks off.

Bud Levine is wearing a pinstriped suit that didn't come off our store racks. Even in gold cuff links and wing tips, he isn't as sure of himself as he appears. I've seen him biting his manicured nails. The cat lady murmurs into her husband's ear, he purrs back and leaves.

Mrs. Levine has a reputation for stalking men behind Mr. Not-So-Sure-of Himself's back. The string of black pearls around her neck cost more than I make in six months. Her eyes are lavender contact lens enhanced and her hair's coiffed a one-length-fits-all. She tucks the back of her designer blouse into a short black leather skirt, smirks at me, and pads off.

At my desk, I can't return to the lined numbers on the page. I'm thinking about Stanley Lassiter. His polite business façade covers up a lot of smoldering heat if I'm any judge. That kiss and groping went to the upper limit on my "Light My Fire" scale.

I had no idea he remembered my name, but he called me Liz. No one calls me Liz. My given name is Elizabeth Anne Butz. To top it off, literally, I'm blessed with large bosoms.

Here's another humiliation — Daddy's a plumber. Butz Plumbing is hard to forget. Mamma hopes for me to have a name-change-by-marriage. Daddy saw on television, in some country, families with marriageable daughters advertise such with red front doors. Ten years after he painted their front door bright enamel red, I'm still unmarried.

At lunchtime, my mouth is full of a double bologna sandwich when Alberta Owens, my best friend says, "Elizabeth, are you going to eat that pickle?" I figure if I let her have my pickle, I can skip telling her about the supply room episode. Stealing my chips, she gossips, "So have you heard the latest? Stanley Lassiter's hot for someone who works here."

I choke on my Coke, "What? Since when?"

"All I know is, he got caught in supply with his sweetie. At least that will put the brakes on Mrs. Levine. I've seen her giving him the eye when he bends over the water fountain." Alberta takes another handful of chips from my deli-plate. "He does have a cute butt, don't you think?" I'm trying to decide whether to keep quiet or spill it. She says, "I bet it's that Phyllis in Sales. What do you think, Elizabeth?"

I'm thinking I can still taste him and know exactly how his body fits mine. I even remember how high my hands have to reach to link behind his neck. "Hmm, it's all gossip. Give it a rest." I get up, "End of quarter, I have to get back to the books."

Back in my office, I notice a voice-mail message blinking on the phone. "Elizabeth, this is Stanley Lassiter. Could you please come to my office — when you have a minute?" I'm holding my breath as I replay it again, three times.

I slip into his office. Now, I notice his nice buns. He's bending over, freeing his canvas briefcase strap caught in his mega-chair wheels. I feel like a kid sent to the principal's office. He straightens and turns when I say, "You wanted to see me? I'm ok about this morning. You'll get no sexual harassment from me." What? He's staring at me.

"I wish it were that easy. Mr. Levine just invited *us*," his emphasis on *us*, "to go to the outer banks next month, Thanksgiving."

I'm not comfortable with a situation that involves an *us*. I say, "I'm sorry, did you invite me to go somewhere with you?"

"Well, Bud and Pricilla Levine have a house at Duck. Now that he thinks we're an item, he invited us out. I'll cover any extra expenses you have. I guess there's a dressy evening thing planned." His invitation causes my stomach to twitch. Or, it may be the double bologna sandwich I ate.

"Mr. Lassiter," I begin. He interrupts.

"Call me Stanley. We'll be spending the weekend together, remember?"

"I don't think so. I don't do weekends with my Vice President of Human Resources." My mouth is saying this but my mind is thinking something else.

"*You* have no choice. Priscilla Levine is creating an uncomfortable situation for me. I'd appreciate your help."

I can't believe he needs a bodyguard. From what I remember, he felt like he could take care of himself. "Can I give you an answer tomorrow?" I'm hedging. I think there's a look of disappointment on his face as I close his office door.

I call in sick the next day. I clean house, dig the goop out of the corner behind the bathroom door with a nail file and an old toothbrush. Wearing flannel shorts and a college t-shirt, I answer the door, gross toothbrush in hand.

"You don't look sick to me." Stanley Lassiter pushes a bouquet of flowers in my face. "You look kind of cute. Can we talk?" He waits patiently. I look down noting his shoe's across my door sill.

"What the heck? Make yourself comfortable." While changing, I lose the gross toothbrush, brush my teeth with a spanking new one, and comb my hair. When I come out, I'm wearing jeans, a bra, and a turtleneck sweater.

He's sitting at my kitchen table chugging a beer. I can't help grinning. "That beer is for garden slugs. How is it?"

Without cracking a smile, he takes another gulp, swirls it in his mouth and swallows. "Not bad, do you feed any slug that shows up?" Is Mr. Lassiter flirting?

"Let's start over," he begins. He tells me about growing up east of Raleigh, on a tobacco farm, a fine occupation twenty years ago. I tell him about home near Wilmington. I describe my folks, even the family business. He smiles, but doesn't laugh. I give him a couple of points.

"Understand," he says, nodding his head. He's drinking another slug beer. It's endearing. "In the meantime, can we be friends?" I admit he seems like a nice guy as we eat delivered pizza and slug beer, pardon the pun. Maybe he started out in sales before moving to HR; at any rate, by the time he leaves I agree to accompany him.

The next couple of weeks go smoothly. Stanley and I smile at each other in the hallways. We eat lunch together in the downtown mall. Hotdogs on the corner shows Stanley's a classy guy. Believe me. There is no sex involved. I try not to think about the possibility.

"So how does it feel to be the talk of the office?" he says with mustard on his chin. "Anything you have to report?"

Pointing to my face, I say, "You have mustard on your chin." He smears it. Now bits of napkin and mustard cling to his noon day shadow. "I drove out to the Outlet Shoppes this weekend and bought a dress. You better like it. You paid for it. The shoes are my contribution."

He walks me back to the office and holds the door for me as Mr. Levine passes. On cue, Stanley brushes a loose curl from my forehead. His hand lingers on my cheek. I grab his hand and pat it. I get nervous when a man's hand goes places uninvited. "See you around, Stanley. I gotta get back to work."

Conversations with my mother by phone make no mention of Stanley. When she asks me if I'm coming home for Thanksgiving, I decline telling her I'm going to the Outer Banks with friends.

Stanley picks me up for the drive to the beach. Crossing the long bridge over to the Banks, my stomach begins to churn. This time I can't blame it on a double bologna sandwich.

Huge water oaks drip with Spanish moss cloaking the driveway up to the Levine house. I picture gardeners draping the trees with the stuff, like Christmas tree decorations. Priscilla Levine preens herself welcoming us, "I'll take you to your room so you can freshen up." She captures Stanley's arm in hers and guides us. It seems to me she's rubbing his arm against her breast, what there is of it. *Ha*!

I take Stanley's hand from hers and rest it on my shoulder while reaching around his waist. I stick a finger in his belt loop and give it a little pull. He notices.

"This is nice, Mrs. Levine," I say. "Feel like a nap, dear." I smile at old Stan and he begins to nibble my ear and softly breathe in it. As Mrs. Levine leaves our room, he starts a bit of serious groping. It gets my motor running. I throw caution to the wind and hope he knows how to undo a multi-hooked brassier with one hand. Stanley's not surprised when she pops her head back to tell us when cocktails begin.

When she finally closes the door, he sighs and turns away. "I knew she'd come back. Can't be a Vice President of Human Resources and not be able to read people." We have a private bathroom and he goes in closing the door. I tug my suitcase up on the bed and begin unpacking. Freshly hand washed, he comes out smelling like designer soap. "Good so far."

"I'm a bit put out." My clothes hang in the humongous armoire and the king-sized bed looks inviting. Four spiral posts hold a delicate canopy above. "Which side do you want?" I say, testing the firmness by jumping up and lying back, eyes closed. Through the crack of my eyelids, I see him nonchalantly go to the other side and stretch out. With the acre of bed between us, I can still feel his body heat.

"I hope you don't snore," he says as he rolls on his side and promptly falls asleep. After fifteen minutes, I get up and carry my makeup bag into the bathroom, shutting the door. I run water into the vintage tub and sink down into chin high bubbles. I'm checking myself out in the overhead mirror when he taps on the door. "We have to be ready in 30 minutes. Are you pacing yourself?" He pokes his head into the room and I answer with a wet loofah. He retreats. His arm returns, waving a white terrycloth surrender flag robe.

"Toss it over. I'll be out in a sec." I reluctantly climb out and slip on the robe. I hear him humming in the next room. When I finally exit, he's pulled on his dress pants and hung his dinner jacket by the door. I never thought sleeveless undershirts were sexy — until now. While he shaves, I dress. My coppery dress shows off my attributes, both of them, nicely. I have to tell you, when he comes out, he's speechless. His eyes slowly take inventory, from the top of my head, around my off-the-shoulder bodice, down the slit-skirt to my sexy heels, which clinch it.

"You clean up pretty good, Butz," he grins slipping on his pleated-front shirt. He turns to tuck in and zip up.

Using my best Southern girl accent, I curtsy, "Why, thank you Mr. Lassiter." I actually flutter my eye lashes as I twirl. On the hour, he offers his arm and we descend into the "jaws of hell."

There are four other couples looking us over. I ignore their scrutiny by scanning the hors d'oeuvre table for eats — no Buffalo wings, smoked weenies, or chips with dip. There's salmon mousse, bacon-wrapped scallops and one large crystal bowl of boiled shrimp.

My Mama once told me the best party person is the one who listens, so the rest of the evening I do. "So how long have you two been an item, honey?" Mr. Levine takes advantage of our Southern endearments, hugging me a bit too warmly as we rise from dinner. I take his arm from around my waist and pat it.

"Now, Mr. Levine," I smile sweetly at Stanley.

Stan eases to my side. "Mrs. Levine suggested we might like to walk over to the beach. Can I get your coat?" He kisses the top of my head before leaving me with the cat lady and the top cat. They smile like Cheshire bookends.

As Mr. Levine's eyes take inventory of my assets, Mrs. Levine leans whispering, "Why don't you get lost after we head out?"

Stanley returns to drape the coat on my shoulders. She watches our every move. Great, my purple quilted nylon windbreaker sets this dress off perfectly. As I shove an arm into the sleeve, I feel his hand skim my breast. He turns me, placing an arm around my waist as he invites Bud to join us. Bud declines.

"Don't leave me," Stanley whispers in my ear. He kisses me on the back of my neck. I swear! If this man read my diary, he couldn't be more precise at hitting all my sensitive spots.

"Did I unknowingly list all my erogenous zones when I took this job?" I flirt at him. Mrs. Levine ignores our nose-to-nose coziness. She stalks ahead.

Away from the house spotlights, the sky glitters like Christmas lights. I hold him tighter. It could be the chill or just my unwillingness to let go. At another time, I might slip off my shoes to huddle down in the sand pulling him around me, like bacon wrapping a scallop.

"Stanley, come. I promise not to bore you," she beckons. Repeating his supply-room maneuver, Stanley's mouth is on mine before I can squeak. I ignore the cat lady's hiss. Still attached to my lips, he reaches beneath my coat and pulls me closer. His hands run over my body like they memorized each curve. I feel myself purring to his touch. Stanley has my full attention. I know exactly how far to reach and link my arms around his neck. He used mouthwash while he was upstairs, silly man. I feel his body tilt into mine."

When we finally come up for air, I'm light-headed, glad he's holding me up. "No one in sight. Was that for real or just show," I ask.

"I could do this and let you feed me slug beer for a long, long time, Liz." He comes in for another lip lock.

Since that weekend, we've shared more a hotdog in the park! When I work up the courage, I'll call Mama. She's gonna be surprised. By New Years, Daddy may need to repaint their front door.

Other books written by Karen E. Dodd:

Carolina Comfort
Down East on Nelson Island

Contact the author for purchase information.

6304 Albatross Drive
New Bern, NC 28560

(252) 514-2953
dkdodd1@cox.net

Printed in the United States
67914LVS00001BA/1-144

9 780970 719720